JB Gill rose to fame as a member of one of the UK's biggest boy bands – JLS. They dominated the charts for five years, boasting five number-one singles, over ten million record sales worldwide and a multitude of awards.

Ten years ago, JB set up a farm in the Kent countryside, where he lives with his wife, Chloe, son, Ace, and daughter, Chiara. Their farm successfully produces award-winning KellyBronze turkeys and free-range Tamworth pork.

Together with his family, JB presents Channel 5's Milkshake TV series *Cooking with the Gills*. He is also the lead presenter on the CBeebies BAFTA-nominated television series *Down on the Farm* and features on Channel 5's *On the Farm* series.

ACE and the ANIMAL HEROES
The Big Farm Rescue

JB GILL

ILLUSTRATED BY
BECKA MOOR

PUFFIN

For my Ace and my Kiki Bear – thank you for the inspiration. And to my Chloe for your belief in me.

PUFFIN BOOKS

UK | USA | Canada | Ireland | Australia
India | New Zealand | South Africa

Puffin Books is part of the Penguin Random House group of companies
whose addresses can be found at global.penguinrandomhouse.com.

www.penguin.co.uk   www.puffin.co.uk   www.ladybird.co.uk

First published 2023
001

Text copyright © JB Gill, 2023
Illustrations copyright © Becka Moor, 2023
Cover photograph © JB Gill, 2023
Interior photograph © Matt Hind, 2023

The moral right of the author and illustrator has been asserted

Typeset in Bembo Infant MT Std, 16/26pt
Text design by Janene Spencer
Printed in Great Britain by Clays Ltd, Elcograf S.p.A.

The authorized representative in the EEA is Penguin Random House Ireland,
Morrison Chambers, 32 Nassau Street, Dublin D02 YH68

A CIP catalogue record for this book is available from the British Library

ISBN: 978–0–241–51446–7

All correspondence to:
Puffin Books, Penguin Random House Children's
One Embassy Gardens, 8 Viaduct Gardens, London SW11 7BW

MIX
Paper from
responsible sources
FSC   FSC® C018179
www.fsc.org

Penguin Random House is committed to a
sustainable future for our business, our readers
and our planet. This book is made from Forest
Stewardship Council® certified paper.

1

Grandparents really are the **BEST** kind of parent. Well, at least that's what Ace Sinclair always told himself and his friends. 'Because grandparents have the word **"grand"** in their title,' he would say in an extremely matter-of-fact tone. And the truth was that Ace's grandparents were the grandest of any of them. They had lived together at Number 11 Helix Gardens in a white house with a royal-blue door since Ace was two years old. He couldn't remember much about his own parents, but Gaga and Gigi had told him so many wonderful stories about them that it didn't seem to matter one bit.

'Gaga' was the first word Ace ever spoke. Nobody could quite believe that he'd said it because Ace's mum had called her own grandfather 'Gaga' when she was little! So Gaga it had always been, and it suited him perfectly.

Before he'd become 'Gaga', Daniel Patrick O'Sullivan had had many different jobs in his seventy-four years of life. He'd been a bricklayer, a firefighter, a driver (although not the racing kind, like Ace's favourite sportsperson, Lewis Hamilton), an insurance broker, a Savile Row tailor and even a florist!

He had retired a total of three times and that meant that he'd received his pension on three different occasions, but Ace still hadn't quite worked out what a pension actually was.

Gaga told the best jokes, but he also had a **terrible** habit of laughing at the punchline before he'd actually finished telling the joke. Nevertheless, Ace would laugh every time because Gaga laughing was always funnier than the joke itself.

Everyone loved Gaga. As soon as he spoke to anyone, they felt like they'd known him for years, and if anybody ever mentioned the word 'Ireland', well, let's just say any chance of sticking to the rest of the day's schedule was pretty much over.

When it came to fashion, Gaga was completely unique and unmissable. You could always find him in a crowd because he insisted on wearing the brightest and loudest shirts for almost every occasion. And today was no exception.

Gaga **bouⁿced** into the kitchen wearing a shirt that was as pink as the inside of a grapefruit, wide open at the collar with the sleeves rolled up to just below the elbows. Gaga sometimes forgot to take his pyjama shorts off before breakfast but today he had donned a pair of pale pink chinos, which, despite being a completely different shade of pink, matched his shirt surprisingly well. On his feet, he wore light brown, furry slippers – a present Ace had bought him for Christmas. He. Felt. **FANTASTIC!** Even if he did look and sound rather like a flamingo.

'*Goooooooooood morning, all! Good morning, all! How are we all on this fine morning!*' he sang at them.

Gaga was a talented man in many ways, but singing was NOT one of his strengths. Before he could blast out another off-key, flamingo-esque tune, Gigi brushed past him like a breath of fresh air on her way to the fridge.

'Morning, Danny boy!' she said to Gaga. She gave Ace a big, sloppy kiss on his forehead as he sat down at the breakfast table and then a mischievous wink, before whispering, 'It looks like someone got up on the right side of bed this morning, didn't they!'

Ace grinned back at her. There seemed to be something special in the air today.

Ace's Gigi was equally as incredible as Gaga. Carmen Judith George was an extraordinarily glamorous woman. She dressed the part, she looked the part, she even smelled the part.

Even though Ace thought she was the grandest of grandmothers, Gigi was very clear that she didn't like being called 'Granny'. Instead she came up with Gigi – one 'G' standing for 'Granny' and the second for her surname, 'George'. It took Ace a while to be able to pronounce it, but the name had stuck and now he never called her anything else.

Gigi loved to travel, and the first entry on her bucket list currently read: '*Visit every country in the world.*' Of course, Gigi hadn't even been to half the countries in the world, but she was a cup-half-full type of person who always looked on the bright side.

She had a brilliant creative mind, and

had been an engineer and an inventor
with business cards that read:

GIGI GEORGE
Innovation Guru
Extraordinaire

But those days were all 'once upon a time',
as she would say.

Gigi was born on a small island in the
Caribbean called Antigua. Ace had never
been, but Gigi would tell him stories of
its 365 beaches (one for every day of the
year!) and how she'd left the beautiful
beaches behind to live in London when
she was only ten – the same age Ace was
now. Her mother had decided to come to
England to train as a nurse after she and

Gigi's father got divorced. Her training meant long and tiring shifts, so Gigi often had to live with friends and relatives when she was little.

She told Ace that she had sometimes felt lonely during those years, but she knew that you had to work hard to achieve your dreams and that her mum was trying to build a better life for them both.

Gigi had studied and built up an engineering empire from scratch. As engineers go, she was the very best of her kind and she often applied those creative and technical skills to everyday life. For example, she developed a recipe for her world-famous spare ribs, which were — according to Google and verified by *all*

of Ace's school friends – the best ribs in the whole world. Her breakfasts had also achieved legendary status.

Speaking of which, Gigi was putting the finishing touches to a perfect stack of six pancakes and, as she set the plate down in front of Ace, his eyes couldn't help but expand to the size of the saucer holding Gaga's cup of tea!

'Gigi!' he said. 'I thought we only had pancakes at the weekend!'

Gigi flashed another of her heart-warming smiles and replied, 'Well, I'm not sure why, but I woke up today feeling like it was a **special occasion**.'

Ace smiled at her, then looked back down at his plate.

'What did you put in them this time?'
he asked. He knew Gigi loved to talk
about her latest culinary inventions.

Gigi returned to flipping pancakes as
she answered. 'Today, I conducted a little
taste test to see which ingredients would
work best with each other. I know you
love lemon and sugar and, of course, those
go so brilliantly because one is bitter and
the other sweet. So I tried out a little kiwi
with some lime that was left over
from last night's dinner,
then some grapefruit
with banana, and then,
finally, blueberries, raspberries
and mint. Why don't you
have a taste and see

which one you think works best?'

Ace grinned as he tucked into his pancakes. He wished he could be just as brilliant as Gigi, but he was really more of an all-rounder. He wasn't the absolute best at anything, but he could be pretty good at almost everything when he was trying his hardest. Gaga said that Ace hadn't quite found what he was best at **yet**, but he was bound to one day.

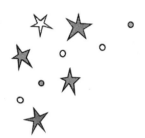

2

It might surprise you to know that Gaga and Gigi weren't married. Gaga was Ace's mum's dad and Gigi was Ace's dad's mum, which sounds complicated but was simplified by the very *unc*omplicated fact that they both adored Ace. Together they made the **perfect team**. Like when Gigi wanted to buy a motorcycle with a jet-activation device to take her to a top speed of 520 mph and Ace reminded Gigi that they needed to ride around the city, not fly. He managed to convince her to settle for two cherry-red Harley-Davidson motorbikes – with matching cherry-red sidecars.

Ace loved riding in Gigi's sidecar. They would whizz down their local high street on a Saturday morning to get their weekly groceries and Gigi always rode really fast, which meant Ace looked like he had been dragged through a hedge backwards by the time they reached their destination.

Every month or so, Gigi and Gaga would get on their motorbikes and take Ace to the nearest farm on the edge of the city. He loved visiting the farm; it was the closest he got to having actual pets.

While Gigi enjoyed going fast, Gaga preferred to take things slowly and enjoy

city culture. He especially loved fashion! One time, he decided to get up from his seat in the front row of a show during London Fashion Week to introduce himself to the designer for an extremely prestigious fashion house to discuss the comeback of the bumbag. Unfortunately the designer mentioned that he had to source all his materials from one particular workshop, which was in – you guessed it – Ireland! Had it not been for Ace taking Gaga firmly by the hand and leading him back to his seat, they might still be standing there talking about the **Emerald Isle**.

So, with Gaga's charm and Gigi's intellect, Ace had learned early on that it was up to him to be the sensible, level-headed one and that's what made them the perfect team.

Ace squirted maple syrup into the dipping bowl Gigi had placed next to his pancakes. He picked up his knife and fork, and cut into the whole stack of six pancakes to make the perfect pizza-slice triangle.

'The proof of the pudding is always in the eating,' guffawed Gaga, between sips of his third tea of the morning.

Ace had heard that saying a million times before, but Gaga was right. His favourite fruits were bananas and grapefruit, and Gigi had blended the perfect mix of banana and grapefruit juice into the pancakes. The taste was **INCREDIBLE**. The tang of the tart grapefruit on his tongue mixed perfectly with the sweetness of overripe banana.

As he continued to munch on his breakfast, he looked up at the big gold clock on the wall and realized that he was going to be late for school. Ace hated being late because it meant he wouldn't be able to play football in the playground with his friends before lessons started, so he began eating at top speed – almost as if he was being powered by a jet-activation device!

As Ace was stuffing the final bit of pancake into his mouth, the doorbell rang. Gigi opened the door and, seeing that it was Chris the postman, greeted him with one of her beautiful smiles.

'Here you go,' said Chris. 'It's a parcel for you, along with a couple of letters that you need to sign for – one's addressed to you and the other's for your Ace. He'll have to open it when he's back from school, I suppose.'

Knowing how much Ace hated being late, Chris was rather surprised to hear Ace half shout, half mumble a 'hwwwwwey qquwwittttthhhh' as he ran out of the kitchen and into the hallway.

'I think you'd better get a move on, don't you? You and me both!' Chris laughed, turning and bouncing down the path before knocking at Number 13.

Ace looked down at the large muddy-brown envelope. He hardly ever received post. Well, except when it was his birthday, and then it was mainly cards, of course. Ace contemplated leaving the letter until he returned home from school, but Gigi (who could be very impatient sometimes) said, 'Oh my, Ace – they're the same! They look very official! Go on – open it now. I'll get you to school in a flash on the motorbike for a change.'

The truth was that Ace was also very curious about the letter, so he sat on the bottom step of the staircase and tore into the envelope that would change his life forever.

As he read the letter, his face scrunched

up in confusion. The words just didn't make any sense. Hoping that Gigi could understand it, he looked up at her to see her face turn a much lighter shade of brown. Her mouth rounded into an 'O' shape before she put a shaking hand over it. Ace started to feel really worried. *What was going on?*

Gaga sensed something was wrong too and made his way into the hallway. 'Are you two OK?'

In a croaky voice, Gigi whispered, '*Ace, dear, you'd better sit down.*'

She'd forgotten that Ace was already sitting down and that it was her who required the seat. She swallowed hard as Gaga brought her a chair.

'This is a letter from our lawyer,' she said with tears in her eyes. 'It's addressed to us both because . . . my half-brother, your great-uncle, Hakim . . . has just died,' Gigi concluded solemnly.

3

Ace had been too young to remember when his parents had died, just as Gigi had been too young to really remember her half-brother, Hakim. He was much older than she was – her father's eldest son from his first marriage – and, because he'd been a highly respected pilot, he'd travelled a lot, so she didn't hear from him regularly, although they had kept in touch through social media.

Gigi sat down at the kitchen table feeling overwhelmed by sadness and memories. She remembered how excited she had been as a little girl when Hakim got his pilot's licence and took her for a ride in his Cessna 152 two-seater aeroplane.

Ace's voice broke through her memories. 'This letter can't be for me though. It's got the name **"Will"** on it,' said Ace, frowning in confusion.

Gaga looked more closely and, placing a hand on Ace's shoulder, he said, 'No, it's not addressed *to* Will; it *is* a will.'

Before he could say any more, Gigi spoke. 'A will is a legal document. Some people write one to make sure that, when they die, their possessions go to their loved ones. Your Great-Uncle Hakim was a pilot and his plane is assumed to have crashed over the Atlantic Ocean.'

Ace handed the document to Gaga. Turning the first page, Gaga read the words out loud:

'*This will is made by me, HAKIM FAROUK AKBAR, of 2223 Appleby Way, Jacksonville, Florida, United States of America. I appoint Carmen Judith George to be my executrix and trustee. I give my estate in Bellevue, Kent, to my great-nephew, Ace Sinclair.*'

Ace's head hurt. 'What does that mean, Gigi?'

Before she could answer, Gaga said, 'Look, Ace, there's another letter attached to the will addressed to you.'

He handed it to Ace, who read it out:

Dear Ace,

How I wish I had taken the time to get to know you in person. Your Gigi has told me so much about you and she says you're the next in line to inherit the great George mind! Lucky boy!

She also mentioned that you love animals and have always wanted a pet of your own. I have a farm in Kent, which I'm now passing on to you. In life, everything is not always as it seems. You should know that my animals are very special . . .

Ace was too shocked to read any more. He passed the letter to Gaga and sat open-mouthed as Gaga digested it, then explained that Ace's Great-Uncle Hakim had left him a six-bedroom farmhouse and several outbuildings in the countryside, and a collection of British pound coins – one for every year since 1920. Gaga paused before reading the last line of the letter aloud.

'*Ace, you will only inherit this property if you choose to assume ownership within one week of receiving this letter!*'

'A week!' Gigi shrieked loudly.

Ace didn't know what to say. He wondered what the farmhouse looked like and who'd been looking after the animals while Great-Uncle Hakim had been away. He felt

bewildered and stunned by the news, but there was also another feeling beginning to glow inside him. He didn't recognize it at first, but as it glowed bigger and brighter he realized what it was. **Excitement!**

Ace had always felt a tiny bit jealous of his best friend, Kevin, who had two dogs – Charlie and Fliss. And Mr Jones from next door had a pet python, which was very cool – but Ace had just inherited an entire farm full of animals!

The excitement bubbling up inside him disappeared, however, when he thought of his friends and his house and just how much he loved living in the city. No more visits to the market and all the stallholders shouting, 'Pound a pound-a 'naaaaanas!'

over and over again. No more birthdays at the IMAX. No more missing their stop on the Tube because Gaga was chatting to commuters. Could he really leave the only place he'd ever called home?

Gaga looked over at Ace and could see his mind working furiously.

'Come on, Ace. It's time for school. We can talk about all this later.'

Gigi was in no fit state to ride after such upsetting news, so it was Gaga's cherry-red sidecar that Ace jumped into. As they zipped along, Ace was so worried about making such a big decision that, for the first time, he didn't even care that he was late for school.

4

Ace spent the morning in a daze. He didn't pay attention in science – his favourite subject. He totally didn't hear when the teacher asked him a question, which led to an awkward silence and Mr Prufrock spending his break time questioning whether there was any way he could make rock formations more interesting. Ace didn't even notice when he picked up Kevin's coat instead of his own as he headed to the playground, leaving Kevin to chase after him down

33

the corridor with a football under one
arm.

'Seriously, Ace, **what's up?** You're like
a super science nerd and today you didn't
even want to look in the magnifying glass!'
Kevin said, trying to catch his breath.

Ace just shrugged. Sensing a real
problem, Kevin threw his free arm round
Ace as they walked outside.

'OK, I tell you what. Let's go get our
crisps and then we'll play football. That'll
sort you out.'

Kevin thought that any problem could be sorted out by twenty minutes of kicking a ball around. Football made *everything* better.

Ace's insides squirmed. He'd been best friends with Kevin since the day they'd started nursery together at three years old. How was he going to break it to his friend of seven years that he might be moving to the middle of nowhere in less than a week?

'Thanks for the offer, man,' said Ace, gently pushing Kevin's arm off his shoulder. 'You go – I'll be along in a minute.'

Kevin didn't need to be told twice and dribbled the football across the playground to a group of boys and girls waiting for him.

5

All Ace had ever known was city life. On his way home from school that day, he took the scenic route and walked through the park. He knew this neighbourhood, this city, this place like the back of his hand. He knew all the best shortcuts to take when he needed to get to the high street, the school, the video-game shop. He knew the areas where it was safe to ride his bicycle in the middle of the road. And he loved spending as much time as

he possibly could in his local park, playing
football or racing his BMX against Kevin
on the specially designed track.

Ace always enjoyed it when Mrs Dix
would get an ice cream for everyone
in the class during the last week of the
summer term, right before they broke up
for the holidays. And the annual fireworks

display on Bonfire Night, when Gaga would hoist him up on to his shoulders to get the best view while Ace sipped on a cup of hot chocolate – that was his favourite.

As he exited the park gates to walk the final stretch to his house, he stopped at the local grocery shop to pick up a Snickers bar and hoped it would pick up his mood too. He also got a Twix for Gigi and a Bounty for Gaga. The shopkeeper tried to

talk to Ace, but he was too distracted by the question going round and round in his head: *Could I be this happy on the farm?*

★

When Ace walked through the front door, his nostrils were not greeted with the usual smell of a delicious dinner, expertly crafted by Gigi. Neither did his grandmother meet him at the door with her customary warm hugs and kisses before telling him to go and take off his school uniform. Instead it was Gaga who was in the hallway.

'Ace, once you've changed, we're going to order pizza for dinner as a special treat.'

Ace could see that Gaga was trying hard to be his usual chirpy flamingo self, but Ace wasn't fooled. Gigi loved cooking!

It made her heart sing – and sing loud. Gigi must be feeling pretty terrible if she didn't want to cook.

As Ace got changed, he realized he was going to have to take control of the situation. Great-Uncle Hakim had chosen him to take over the farm – he must have had a good reason for that.

By the time Ace was wearing his favourite football shirt and heading down the stairs for dinner, he'd made up his mind.

6

Ace sat down to dinner feeling excited, but he couldn't help noticing that Gaga and Gigi were very quiet. So quiet, in fact, he could have heard a pin drop.

'OK. So it's clear that this news is pretty mind-blowing, but everything's going to be fine,' he said, a little more confidently than he really felt. 'There must be a reason Great-Uncle Hakim left me his farm and I think we should find out why.'

Both his grandparents stared at him in shock. Never in their wildest dreams had they imagined themselves living outside the city.

'I mean,' continued Ace, unfolding a piece of paper with his list of reasons for going, 'let's look at the positives. Bigger house. Lots of animals. More space. Lots of animals. Fresh air. Lots of animals. Come on – those are **pretty great reasons**. You know how much I've always wanted a pet. I'm ready for the responsibility *and* we'll finally have the space for one.'

'But – but – but where am I going to get all the ingredients I need for cooking?' said Gigi.

Ace knew why she was worried about this. The three of them had been on

holiday to the countryside last summer
and stayed in the New Forest. They often
cooked their own food when on a holiday
and, while Gigi had managed to rustle
up delicious meals all week, she did end
up more and more frustrated by the fact
that there weren't the usual variety of
ingredients on offer that she was used to.
The owner of the local greengrocer's just
looked at her with a blank face when she'd
asked him whether he
had any cassava,

which she wanted to go into a new vegetarian dish she was trying. She'd been relieved to get back home to her own kitchen, with all her Caribbean herbs, spices and ingredients.

'Well . . . well,' stuttered Ace, 'we'll just have to get things delivered . . . i–i–instead of going to the shops.'

'Ace, I like your enthusiasm, but I'm just not sure it will work,' said Gaga. 'It's not going to be fun living in the middle of nowhere, without any real neighbours for miles.'

Ace knew how much Gaga loved the Joneses who lived next door at Number 13. He couldn't deny that they were great neighbours.

45

Without any children of their own, the Joneses were always more than happy to look after Ace when both Gaga and Gigi were out for the evening. They always let him eat ice cream, even after he'd already had dessert, and Mr Jones had taught him everything he knew when it came to playing chess. They also put on a great barbecue or two every summer, which the whole road was invited to. Ace could see that Gaga was worried that there wouldn't be anyone to speak to out in the countryside.

'Yes, but . . . but . . . there will still *be* neighbours – there has to be!' Ace replied. 'And just think – you'll get to wear all your Barbour jackets and fit right in!'

Gaga still wasn't convinced.

'I'm inclined to agree with Gaga – sorry, Ace,' Gigi added.

This was not good. It hadn't gone to plan at all! Ace finished his pizza and silently helped Gigi tidy up the kitchen before he headed upstairs for a bath and bed. He couldn't help feeling that it would take a miracle to get Gaga and Gigi out of the city.

7

The next morning, as Ace brushed his teeth, his mind was whirring.

'Right, let's make a plan,' Ace said to himself. 'First, I'll tell Kevin. If he's on board, he can always help me convince Gigi and Gaga if I need him to.' He did up the top button of his school shirt to make sure it fitted snugly. 'It feels like the right thing to do, and Gigi always says to "trust your gut".'

★

As Ace entered the school gates, Kevin rushed up to him, dribbling a football.

'Hey, mate, you in a better mood today?'

Ace smiled. 'Yeah, but I do have something big to tell you.'

But Kevin wasn't listening – he was already running towards the playground. Ace groaned internally. He really hoped this wouldn't be a hard sell. He'd learned what *not* to say after his conversations with his grandparents the night before and he wanted his friend to see this as an exciting adventure, which is exactly what Ace thought it would be.

In between bicycle kicks and slide tackles, he relayed the big news to Kevin.

BOSH!

'So yesterday I found out I have a great-uncle . . .' began Ace.

49

SLIIIIIDE!

'Aww, cool! What's he like?' replied Kevin, running away to take a corner kick.

'Well . . . he died . . . He was quite – UGH – old . . .' said Ace, jumping up for a header and missing the goal narrowly. 'But he's left me my very own farm with loads of space and animals, and told us we have to move there next week.'

Kevin, in the middle of shielding the ball from their friend Gavin, stopped in his tracks and put his foot on the ball. 'Wait,' he said. 'So you've got your own farm? And you're moving there *next week*?'

Uh-oh. The moment of truth.

'Yep,' said Ace. 'Pass! I'm in!'

He nervously waited for Kevin's

response and a perfectly passed ball. He got neither – good job he wasn't holding his breath. Kevin did a flawless Cruyff turn and ran towards the goal before slotting it into the bottom left corner on his weakest foot.

'OH MY DAAAYS!!!!!!!'

he shouted.

Ace wasn't sure whether this was a reaction to the goal or to the news that he'd just broken. Kevin was definitely smiling, but he hadn't actually said anything that gave away his thoughts.

'Bro, that is super cool!' Kevin said. 'You're gonna have your own animals and everything! You'd better let me come visit whenever I want . . . Ah, man, I wish I had a great-uncle to leave ME a farm!' He ran off after the ball, shouting, 'Imagine having your own football pitch in your garden! No one telling you to watch out for the windows! **Sick!**'

Ace smiled. It felt good having his best friend onside.

The combination of football and Ace's exciting news proved too much for Kevin. **'GUYS!** Guys, Ace has a braaaand-new farm, with loads of animals and about twenty fields as big as football pitches! Shotgun the first visit *obviously* but I'm sure we can all come, can't we, Ace?'

The whole playground filled with excited chatter as Ace's classmates

discussed the possibility of a visit to Ace's new farm. Ace grinned at his best mate.

'**Cheers, Kev,** trust you to blab all my business!' he said.

'Well, you didn't say not to tell anyone!' Kevin replied, as the bell rang to start the day, and they grabbed their bags and headed to their classroom.

★

Unbeknown to Ace, Gaga had been thinking about the letters from Hakim overnight and about whether he and Gigi should consider what Ace had said to them both over dinner. Ace had always had good instincts when it came to these things. Still, it was a pretty bold step for them to move away from everything they knew.

Gaga sat at the kitchen table and looked down at his to-do list for the week. He was just about to put the kettle on for his fourth tea of the morning when the power went out.

'AAAAAARGH!'

Gigi's scream from the basement rang out so loud it made Gaga jump off his seat and roll on to the floor. While he was still trying to stand up, a furious Gigi marched into the room clutching a power tool and wearing a face shield to protect her from the sparks.

'AGAIN,' she said in a shrill voice. 'That's the eighth time in the last six weeks!'

With a huff, Gaga said, 'I wonder what

excuse the electricity company will have for us today!'

He went to pick up the phone to find out when everything would be back on before realizing that wouldn't work either. He groaned.

'Maybe it would be better at your brother's farm! Not so many people using up all the power!'

Gigi wasn't paying much attention to Gaga's grumbling, but his words weren't lost on her. She couldn't help but think that perhaps Gaga – and Ace – were right; they should consider the move. Was it a bad idea or were they just scared of such a big change?

★

Over the next few days, things went from bad to worse. One night, the whole house was woken up by the sound of sirens and helicopters at 2 a.m. – they were following an escaped criminal! Between them, Gigi, Gaga and Ace hardly slept a wink.

A couple of days later, there was a massive ten-car crash at the end of their road! Thankfully, nobody was seriously injured, but two fire engines, three ambulances and five police cars were called to the scene, and the traffic on the surrounding roads was unbearable. Gigi had to cancel her dentist appointment *and* the hairdresser because even she couldn't get through on her Harley-Davidson.

By the end of the week, Gaga and Gigi were absolutely fed up and had decided that Ace might be right after all – it was time for a change.

When they told Ace they'd decided to move to the farm, he **whooped** and **hollered** and jumped into Gigi's arms, almost knocking her off her chair! Gaga and Ace started dancing round

the kitchen, but Gigi brought them back down to earth quickly.

'Do you realize that this means we've only got the weekend to get the whole house packed up and ready to go?'

8

Friday's a good day to finish school on, thought Ace.

They had fish and chips in the lunch hall, followed by double PE, and Mr Telford even let them play football instead of doing exercises in the gym because it was almost the weekend. Mrs Dix threw a farewell party for Ace at the end of the day. She put music on, got the board games out and dished out huge slices of homemade chocolate cake, although Samira did find a guinea-pig hair in hers.

While Ace was enjoying hairy chocolate cake at school, Gigi was starting to panic in the hallway at home, wondering how on earth she was going to get the house packed up in time.

I'm going to have to use extreme measures, she thought to herself, heading down to the basement.

Within three hours, Gigi managed to invent a new contraption called the Dynamic Packer, or Dyna-Packer for short.

It was composed of mechanized bits and
pieces (including a mini conveyor belt),
with an entrance and an exit on either
side. She placed an old box at the exit
and one of Gaga's pink jumpers that had
just finished drying at its entrance. Then
she stepped back to watch it work. The
jumper was immaculately folded by the
arms with hooks as it travelled through
the body of the machine, landing in the
box with a soft **plop**.

'Hmmm,' Gigi said, frowning at the
three Dyna-Packers in front of her.
'You're going to have to go a lot faster
than that!'

She cranked the speed up on each
machine. Leaving piles of clothes, shoes,

books and household gadgets in front of them, she let them whirr to life, packing everything neatly and efficiently.

'Time for a cup of tea, I think,' said Gigi, heading up the basement stairs with a spring in her step.

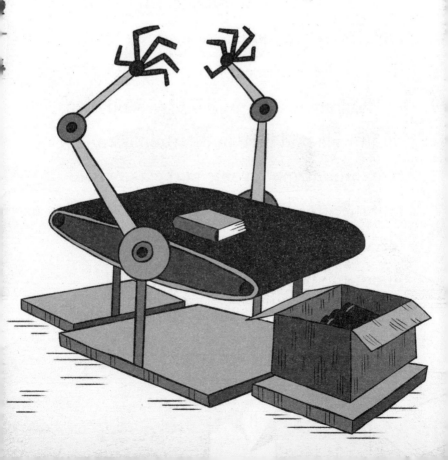

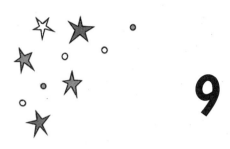

9

'More sausages, Ace?' Mr Jones roared, tipping another five sausages on to his plate, even though Ace was so full he thought he might explode.

The Joneses had promised to send them off in style and they had certainly done that, organizing an epic barbecue where half the street had popped over to say farewell – and to sample Gigi's world-famous spare ribs.

It was a welcome break after a crazy Friday of non-stop packing and tidying and arranging. Thankfully, the Dyna-Packers had proven to be exceptionally efficient so they had just about finished in time – although there was quite a lot of cursing from Gaga when he realized he'd accidentally packed every single pair of underpants and couldn't remember which box they were in.

Between everyone at the barbecue, there were more tears (mostly from Gigi) and laughter (mostly from Gaga) than one of those really mushy romantic comedies that your parents love watching and you hate sitting through. Tomorrow was the first day of a brand-new adventure, but they were all going to miss their friends and neighbours.

Saturday morning was bittersweet. Gigi treated everyone to scrambled eggs and honey on toast, served on paper plates because the proper ones were packed away in one of the hundred boxes being lifted into the removal van.

Gaga ran around the house, flapping like a distressed flamingo, trying to make sure they had absolutely everything, while Gigi went to fire up the motorcycles. Ace heard Gaga bounding down the stairs and grabbed his rucksack.

'All clear, Ace,' said Gaga. 'Time to say goodbye!'

The words seemed so final but there was no backing out now.

Kevin's mum had brought him over, as promised, as soon as his football training had finished to say goodbye and, as Ace walked out, he went straight over to hug his best friend.

'Gonna miss you, mate,' Kevin said, kicking the ball against the wall while Gaga spoke to his mum and Gigi waited

for the removal people to secure all their belongings tightly in the van. 'I mean, who's gonna give me those killer passes to set me up on goal?'

Ace laughed and joined in the ball-kicking against the wall.

'You'll just have to go all the way yourself!' he said. 'In any case, I'll come back in the holidays or maybe you could come visit me for a few days if you don't have football camp.'

Ace knew he'd miss Kevin terribly, but he also knew he was one of those friends who was more like a brother. Even if they didn't see each other for ages, they would always be there for each other.

'Say cheese!' said Mrs Jones. She

was standing next to her husband and smiling.

Ace, Gigi and Gaga huddled together and smiled back as Mrs Jones took a picture of the three of them standing on the drive outside 11 Helix Gardens for the last time.

Kevin passed Ace his helmet before doing a rainbow flick with the ball over his head.

'See you around, mate!'

One sidecar was full to the brim with all the odds and ends they couldn't fit into the house-moving van. The other sidecar's comfortable leather seat was waiting for Ace to assume his position. After one last look at their friends and the house he'd called home for just over eight years, he

gave a heavy sigh and slid on his helmet
with an audible **plunk**.

Then they were off!

★

'Are we there yet?' Ace shouted over the
rattling grumble of the traffic.

The journey to First Fruits Farm was
taking forever. They were heading to the

quirky village of Bellevue in Kent. It was only about fifty-five miles outside London, but there were so many winding roads through the countryside that it was taking much longer than expected. Ace had no idea where they were and was starting to feel a little queasy, not to mention bored. He resigned himself to counting red trucks and only realized he'd dozed off when he was woken with a gentle poke in the shoulder by Gaga.

'Wake up, sleeping beauty – we're here now,' Gaga said, humming.

The sky had darkened during the trip and Ace rubbed the sleep out of his eyes before looking around him. He was surrounded by space and trees and more space and more trees and, right in the middle of all that space and all those trees, was the farmhouse.

The long snaking drive was bordered on both sides by a front garden bigger than the whole house in Helix Gardens. Ace's first thought was that Kevin would not be disappointed – he could build his own football pitch here **three times over!**

He climbed out of the sidecar and took off his helmet. This was it! The moment he had been waiting for. He was nervous but also excited. As he gazed up at the house, he couldn't help but notice that it looked older and more run-down than he'd expected – and then he remembered that Great-Uncle Hakim hadn't been there for some time.

Inside the house, everything was coated in inch-thick dust and smelled musty and damp – the kind of smell you get when you've had your sports kit wrapped up in your schoolbag for the whole of the summer holidays.

He looked into the kitchen and could see two smashed windows next to the back door. The light bulb was missing, and the door itself looked like it might fall off its hinges at any moment.

Ace decided to explore upstairs. He couldn't help but notice how much the floorboards creaked and groaned beneath his feet. At the top of the stairs, he opened the first door on his right.

'AAAAAAAaaaargggggggh!'

Ace's scream was so loud it could have burst eardrums. His heart was beating like a hummingbird's wings, his face was full of terror, and he leaned against the wall to catch his breath before realizing it was covered in cobwebs.

'**Gah!**' he shouted, flailing his arms around, trying to shake off the sticky threads of the webs. Something had flown at him from the corner of the room and he soon worked out the black shape flapping around his head was a bat!

'**Gagaaaaaaa ...!**' Ace called frantically.

Gaga bounded up

the stairs to Ace's rescue, but they were so rickety that Gaga put his foot right through the top stair.

'**AAAAAAA**aaaargggggggh! Gigi! Heeeeelp!' screamed Gaga.

'What on earth is going on up here?' Gigi said as she climbed the staircase, trying not to laugh at the spectacle that was before her.

Ace was cowering on the only part of the landing that *didn't* have cobwebs on it and Gaga, having freed his foot from the step, was now rolling around on the floor, groaning.

'I think . . . we might need to go . . . to the hospital,' he said. 'I can't stand up.'

Oh dear, Gigi thought to herself.

Oh dear indeed. They'd not even been in the house for thirty minutes and it was already a disaster. Gigi fired up Gaga's motorbike and, with Ace's help, managed to sit him on the back of it. To make matters worse, as she went to pull the front door of the farmhouse shut, the handle came off in her hand. She didn't dare tell the boys in case they refused to return and hoped that she'd be able to open it later on.

★

When they eventually returned from the hospital and had a little something to eat, Gigi put one of the Dyna-Packers to good use. By bedtime, Ace was grateful he at least had somewhere comfy to sleep, but he couldn't help but feel deflated. Gaga and Gigi looked like he felt. They'd hardly said a word since they'd arrived back home and, after an unusually muted goodnight exchange between the three of them, Ace was too exhausted to do anything except brush his teeth and fall into bed.

10

The next morning, Ace awoke at 5 a.m. to the sound of **'COCK-A-DOODLE-DOOOOOOOO!'**

Sitting bolt upright in his bed, he muttered, 'What on earth was that?!'

After another sharp, shrill blast of **'COCK-A-DOODLE-DOOOO!'**, he jumped up out of bed and ran down the corridor, screaming.

'Gaga, Gigi, heeeelp – we're being invaded! **Aaaaaaaargghhh!**'

Ace ran head first into Gaga, who had just stumbled out of his room and was pulling on his 'Super Gaga' dressing gown.

'What was that noise, Gaga? Why was it so loud? I thought we were being attacked, but it was coming from the farmyard. Are we going to be OK?'

Poor Gaga looked like *he* was the one being attacked! Gigi, who slept lightly at the best of times, came running out, holding her hands over her ears.

'It's OK, Ace,' she said. 'Fancy a cockerel giving you such a fright!'

'That . . . was a cockerel?' asked Ace, somewhat bemused. Ace was very familiar with the *words* 'cock-a-doodle-doo' – he'd read the phrase many times in multiple books. He even knew that a cockerel was a male chicken. What he didn't realize was that a human 'cock-a-doodle-doo' and a cockerel's 'cock-a-doodle-doo' are two *very* different sounds!

'Well, we're awake now, so we might as well have some breakfast and then you can go and check out the farmyard,' said Gigi.

'OK, Gigi, sounds like a plan.' Ace ran back down the corridor, towards his room.

'*Last one to breakfast gets the rotten eggs!*' he sang, as he ducked into his wardrobe to fish out his clothes for the day.

Unfortunately it was Ace who was last.

In daylight, the kitchen didn't look *quite* as bad as it had seemed the previous night. The windows at the back door were broken, but it was actually quite a bright, cheery room, in a rickety old farmhouse kind of way. It was a far cry from the neatness of 11 Helix Gardens, but they were here now and determined to make the most of it.

Gigi had laid all the eggs they'd brought with them on the sideboard by the fridge and was getting the bread out to make toast when, quick as a flash, a zip of black flew through the room. The room was turned upside down. There were eggs and bread in the air, the spatula had jumped out of the frying pan, and apple juice flowed out on to the floor as the glass holding it smashed everywhere. Worse still, Gaga's pinstripe shirt was now covered in egg, which was beginning to seep through the material. The rest of the eggs had splattered on the floor.

'What on earth was that?' asked Gaga, fumbling around for something to wipe himself with.

'I think it was a cat!' said Ace, who thought he'd seen the end of a tail as the animal sprang out through one of the broken windows.

Gigi had had quite a fright. Thankfully, this time no one was hurt.

'My goodness,' she said when she'd finally collected herself. 'Well, at least it wasn't a rat . . .'

She burst out laughing and both Ace and Gaga couldn't help but join in.

Once they'd calmed down, their minds turned back to breakfast. Ace's stomach growled and he heard the cockerel screeching from outside again. 'This farm has chickens, right?' he said. 'Maybe they'll have laid some eggs this morning.'

'What's that, Ace?' said Gaga, distracted by the mess on his shirt, especially now that Gigi was trying to clean it off and somehow making the stain worse.

Thinking it might be worth getting out of the kitchen before Gaga had a total meltdown, Ace slipped out of the kitchen door.

As he walked down a winding path towards the farmyard, he could see how run-down the farm actually was. Paving stones were missing, and there were gates and fencing posts that hadn't been replaced in so long they'd gone rotten in the ground – they were probably full of earthworms and bugs.

The path led to a farmyard that was flanked by a small, fenced pasture on each side. At the end of the path was a five-bar gate, which opened up to reveal a U-shaped stable block to the right, which was made up of six stables, a hay barn and a workshop.

On the opposite side of the farmyard was a gate that led to more pasture. Ace followed the fence to the left and came to a mouldy-looking greenhouse – which was as long as the height of Number 11 Helix Gardens! And right in front of its entrance was a lopsided old tractor. Ace ventured past the tractor and found a large area of hard ground that was fenced off – and it looked like the ground was covered with sand. How strange!

Ace turned round and noted the big side gate opposite the greenhouse entrance, which led to a country lane. Next to the tractor was the gate that led back to the main farmyard. Ace went through it and explored behind the stable block. There he found a big, round, fenced-off enclosure where the chickens lived inside their coop. He could hear chickens flapping around furiously inside it. He followed the path past the chickens and came to an orchard next to a small woodland area. The orchard was full of pear trees, cherry trees and apple trees, judging by the rotten fruit on the ground!

Everywhere he looked, Ace could see something that needed fixing. He questioned whether Great-Uncle Hakim had ever actually been to the farm and then he wondered whether he and his grandparents had bitten off way more

than they could chew.

Ace made his way back towards the farmyard. There was a cacophony of noise from what sounded like an extremely out-of-tune choir of farm animals!

There was a whiff of something too, something that smelled really disgusting and he couldn't quite put his finger on where it was coming from. As he rounded the corner to face the stables, Ace saw – or rather smelled – that the whiff was coming from an odd-looking man, who was leaning into one of the stables and looking at the excitable piglets tumbling over each other.

He smelled like Brussels sprouts you've left in your lunchbox that slipped

off the back seat of your mum's car
to underneath the driver's seat and
accidentally flipped open on the hottest
day of the year. **Revolting.** Or like
a skunk that's eaten a vindaloo curry
and then suffered a bout of the runs
inside a one-person lift that only stops
at the hundredth floor of a building.
Disgusting! The pungent smell became
stronger the closer Ace got to the man.

'Hello . . . er, I'm Ace. We've just moved
here. Are you the farm manager?' Ace
said, trying to put on an air of confidence.
Gaga had taught him that first impressions
were incredibly important, so he always
tried to be as bold and as brave as he
could when introducing himself.

The gentleman straightened up abruptly and dusted down his expensive-looking suit. He also wore a grey overcoat, a flat cap and held a walking stick in his left hand. His walking stick was made of ebony and was exceptionally shiny. It had the head of an eagle in silver on its end.

The man had quite a nice face as faces go. It was one of those faces that was incredibly photogenic because everything was in perfect proportion. His eyes were shielded behind square, dark-framed glasses that looked as expensive as his suit. His long, straight nose sat neatly in the middle of his face, and his mouth was an equal distance between that and his dimpled chin. He was clean-shaven so the outline of his jaw gave a look that he meant business.

He looks much better than he smells, thought Ace, as he waited for the man to respond.

In an instant, the symmetry of the man's face was completely disrupted as his nose crinkled and inched upwards, his eyes narrowed and looked perfectly ghastly, while his mouth scrunched into a sneer.

'Well, Ace, I am Henry Crabbington the Third, Councillor Crabbington to you – the local councillor of Bellevue!' He paused here as if expecting a round of applause, but, seeing that none was forthcoming, he continued, looking down his nose at Ace. 'Who is the proprietor of this establishment?'

Ace thought he might faint from the bad stench that clung to Councillor Crabbington, but he didn't want to be rude, so he replied, 'Well, Councillor, I've no idea what a proprietor is, but if it's anything to do with the farm you can talk to me.'

The councillor looked irritated. 'Who is the owner of the farm?'

'I am,' said Ace with a broad smile.

'Don't be ridiculous! You're just a child,' Crabbington retorted.

Ace shrugged. 'That's true, but the farm's still mine. It was left to me in my great-uncle's will.'

Councillor Crabbington took a moment to examine Ace's innocent expression before deciding that he wasn't lying to him.

'Well, well, well, this could be interesting! Very interesting indeed. Perhaps easier than I thought!' (He had meant to say the last part in his head.)

'What's easier than you thought?' Ace asked.

'Oh, nothing! Never you mind, young man!' Councillor Crabbington replied hastily. 'I'm just here to give you this letter.

97

Very important information in here,' he said, tapping the envelope vigorously with the top of his walking stick. 'Make sure you read it.'

Ace didn't like the fact that Councillor Crabbington was smirking as he said this. Why did he look so pleased with himself and why was he cackling away as he walked out of the farmyard gate? Ace was pretty sure only evil villains did that.

He tore open the envelope and, as he read, his mouth formed a silent 'O'. The more he read, the bigger his mouth became. By the time he had finished reading, his mouth was as wide as a tractor wheel and his face was as grey as a white bedsheet that hasn't been washed in months.

To whom it may concern,

It has come to our attention
that this property has changed
ownership and, as such, a customary
inspection is in order. By law,
the inspection is intended to take
place thirty days from the date
of this letter. Upon the property
passing or failing the inspection,
it shall be decided by independent
adjudicator whether the property
will remain under the ownership of
its current proprietor or be sold
to the highest bidder. Please be
advised that nothing further is
required from you at this point and
we look forward to being welcomed
to the farm in due course.

Kind regards,
Councillor Henry Crabbington
the Third

Before the dust had settled from the wheels of the councillor's vintage forty-year-old Mercedes, Ace had sprung into action. He looked in every stall of the stable block and made a mental note of all the things that needed to be fixed.

There was good news and bad news. The good news was that the pens and beds all seemed to be pretty clean, so someone had definitely been tending to the animals. He counted one sow, one boar, six little piglets, three very squawkative hens, one rather flamboyant cockerel, two goats, one cow and a donkey that looked very dispirited.

The bad news was that there was a LOT of work to be done, and thirty days was nowhere near enough time for him to do it. Ace made another note to remind himself that the stable roof needed to be replaced and that the workshop and hay barn both needed a refresh.

By the time he had finished checking everything over, his energy had subsided and given way to frustration and misery. There were hunks of junk lying around without any purpose. The tractor had a puncture. Leaning on the remains of a ride-on lawnmower was an obscure-looking machine, and there were ladders and plastic pipes and bits of scaffolding everywhere.

Ace was starting to feel very homesick

for the neat, orderly house in Helix
Gardens, which didn't smell of petrol and
poo. It suddenly felt very far away.

11

BANG!

Ace was snapped out of his gloomy mood by a loud noise coming from behind the hay barn. He went to take a closer look and was confronted by what he could only describe as a sight to behold.

Standing before him was a girl about his age wearing a pair of dusty old wellies and a pink-and-green flowery dress. What most struck Ace was her hair. It was incredibly long: straight at the top but with a wicked little flick at the end of each lock.

103

She dusted her palms off on her dress before they came to rest on her hips, then, with a flash of anger in her eyes, she said, 'I positively loathe that man!'

Ace just blinked. He couldn't agree more, but his mouth wasn't yet able to say it.

'The name's Bear,' she said, sticking a mud-stained hand right in front of Ace's astonished face. Reluctantly Ace shook her dirty hand.

'I've been looking after your animals ever since Mr Hakim went away,' she said. 'Sorry to hear about your great-uncle, by the way – he was going to teach me how to fly! I'm going to be a pilot when I'm older, or maybe a vet. I haven't decided yet. Anyway, I pretty much spend all my free time here with the animals. When I'm not at school, of course. Hopefully that won't have to change now that we're going to be best friends.'

The stream of words suddenly stopped, and Ace's brain whirred as he tried to process everything this strange girl had just said. Where did he even begin?

Plucking one of the many questions out of his brain, he asked, 'Is your name actually Bear?'

'Briony Elizabeth Amelia Rogers is my full name, but my friends call me Bear. Best friends have no choice. Anyway, you have bigger things than my name to worry about if you don't want Councillor Crabbington to steal this farm.'

'So what's the story with Crabbington then?' Ace said, as he walked over to the donkey with Bear. 'Has he always been like that? And what *is* that smell that follows him around?'

Bear leaned over a stable door to stroke the donkey.

'Rule number one: **never, ever** call him Crabbington. It's *Councillor* Crabbington to the likes of us, otherwise we'll live to regret it. Rule number two: although he is – and always will be – top of my list of things I detest the most, he's the most powerful man around here, so it pays to keep him happy.'

Bear was now walking around as if she was on a mission. Ace followed her, looking a bit like a lost puppy, but he'd already realized it was probably best to just go with the flow where Bear was concerned.

Bear continued. 'Rule number three: the less time you spend with him, the better. You'll do your nostrils a favour, trust me. Either that or invest in a face mask or something. I'm nine and a half, and, as far back as I can remember, Councillor Crabbington has always smelled like that. Rumour has it he fell into the Rotten Reservoir once and has never been the same since.'

Ace was about to ask what the Rotten Reservoir was, but Bear was still going with her never-ending list of rules.

'Rule number four: Councillor Crabbington is a very clever man – that's how he became so powerful. So, if you want to outwit him and pass that inspection, you're going to need to get your thinking cap on. And –' she stopped abruptly, causing Ace to bump into her unexpectedly – 'you'd better run

every single little detail by

me,' she said, pointing her finger straight at his nose. There was a razor-like edge to her voice. 'I'll make sure the plan is bulletproof,' Bear said, relaxing her face into a grin. 'Anything you need, just let me know and I'll help.'

And, with that, Bear walked briskly out of the gate, waving until she was gone.

Ace was left feeling like he'd just been caught up in a tornado, spun round a hundred times and then spat out into a field. He didn't even know how to begin processing all the information he'd just received. He thought about how bold and confident she was and her decision that they would be best friends straight away.

He couldn't believe that he'd managed to make an enemy and a best friend on his first morning on the farm – before he'd even had breakfast! Life in the countryside was a lot more fast-paced than he had been expecting.

Halfway back to the farmhouse, Ace realized he had forgotten to look for eggs. He ran to where he could hear the cluck of the chickens and frantically searched for some without any luck. With all the unusual activity of the day, the hens had forgotten to lay and, instead, sat busily

 preening their feathers and clucking at each other.

As Ace stomped back through the farmyard gate towards the house, he stopped dead in his tracks. Right in front of him on the path was a rather regal-looking cat – black as night but with white paws that made it look like it was wearing ankle-high boots. Although Ace didn't usually believe in superstitions, Gaga had always said that it was bad luck for a black cat to cross your path, so he tried to force the cat to move.

'**Shoo, cat!** Move!' Ace said.

Nothing worked. The cat just stared back at him before it began licking one of its white paws.

'I don't have time for this,' Ace fumed.

Thankfully, as he continued his march

towards the cat, it made an about-turn
and disappeared behind the stables.

★

Gaga had his music blasting while he
sat at the table, cup of tea in hand,
patiently waiting for Gigi to put the
finishing touches to breakfast. Gigi was
so in tune with everything culinary that

she barely had to look at a kitchen or cooking space before she felt comfortable working in it. Although everything was still unfamiliar and the Dyna-Packers hadn't yet unpacked all the utensils, she'd managed to clear up the mess enough to get breakfast going.

'Where on earth did you get to, Ace? You've been ages!' Gaga remarked.

'Please tell me you found some eggs at least?' Gigi asked hopefully.

Without answering either of his grandparents, Ace simply replied, 'I've got a LOT to fill you in on.'

'After breakfast,' said Gigi. 'Your Gaga's only had three cups of tea so far this morning and if he doesn't eat in the next five minutes, he'll probably faint.'

Twenty minutes later, when Gaga had eaten five slices of toast and was feeling much more human, Ace told them all about his recent discoveries.

'You won't *believe* what happened! I went looking for the eggs and this place is a real mess and there's poo *everywhere* and then there was this very odd man who told me that we have thirty days to fix the farm up or it'll be taken away from us! It's all in here,' Ace said, removing the now-crumpled letter from his pocket and placing it on the table.

'Then this girl just appeared out of nowhere and told me *she* was the one who'd been looking after the animals for

Great-Uncle Hakim and that she'd help me if I needed help because she knows **EVERYTHING** and I know nothing and then she disappeared and I don't even know where she lives or how to find her if I need her, plus she talks a LOT and –'

Have you ever said so much in one breath that you went blue in the face? Ace would have done just that if Gigi hadn't interrupted him!

'Ace, dear,' she said, closing the door to the grill and throwing a comforting arm round him, 'calm down and breathe.'

But Ace was on a roll. 'And there weren't any eggs *and* the worst thing about that man is that he stinks. I mean, *really* stinks.'

Gaga, who'd stayed silent throughout Ace's little tirade, didn't mean to laugh, but a little chuckle escaped his lips. He put down his cup of tea, abruptly stood up and announced: 'I know what will make this all better! **A good dance!**'

With that, he promptly turned up the volume on Pharrell Williams' 'Happy', grabbed Ace by the hand and proceeded to prance about the kitchen until the song came to an end. By that point, Ace's mood had completely lifted. Gigi put a hand on his shoulder and gave him a smile, before placing his breakfast down in front of him.

'Seeing as we've got no eggs for the time being, I've made us bacon

sandwiches with a maple-syrup-and-
vanilla-infused brown sauce drizzled over
the top. Eat up, Ace – it'll help you come
up with your plan,' she said.

Gigi, as always, was right. Ace's mind
began plotting a way to fix up the farm
as he tucked into the delicious feast Gigi
had put together.

12

Ace crunched his way through his sandwich on autopilot.

With two bites left, he looked up at Gaga and said, 'OK, Gaga, how about you're in charge of the farm buildings and getting them up to scratch for the animals?'

'Yes, sir,' Gaga replied, giving a mock salute to Ace in the process.

Gaga hadn't unpacked his clothes yet, so his outfit was rather randomly put together. He had on a green, red, white and brown patterned scarf, pale pink chinos, the white trainers he'd travelled in the day before and a sky-blue T-shirt with the words 'Eat, Sleep, Farm, Repeat' embroidered on the front, which he'd been given as a going-away present by Mr Jones. As it was, Ace was so used to Gaga's weird and wonderful outfits that he turned to Gigi without further comment.

'Gigi, do you reckon you could fix all the faulty farm machines or even convert some of them to help us repair the stable roof and tidy all the mess in the yard before the inspection happens?'

Gigi had a worried look on her face.

'I'm not sure, to be honest. It sounds like it'll be quite a task, but I'll certainly do my best to come up with something,' she replied.

She reached across the wooden breakfast table that had been set up temporarily until they had the time to go furniture shopping. Her hand found Ace's and he beamed back at Gigi.

'And see if you can do anything about the smell . . .' said Ace, scrunching up his face. 'Between Bear and me, we'll make sure the animals are well fed, with plenty of water to drink and anything else we can think of. If they're happy, we'll be much happier too.' Despite his lack of experience,

Ace possessed a lot of natural wisdom. 'Good! Come on then, Gaga!' he shouted over his shoulder as he walked out of the back door.

★

Ace wondered when Bear would turn up next, but this thought was pushed out of his mind a second later as he turned the corner of the stable block and was faced with a very chaotic farmyard. Two fully grown Tamworth pigs were running towards him and Gaga – grunting! Ace jumped out of the way with a squeal.

Following the pigs were a troupe of tiny piglets.

They must have escaped from their pen, Ace thought. *These buildings really do need fixing.*

It soon became clear that Ace and Gaga had no clear strategy for catching the piglets, who were much quicker than either of them could have imagined. After running round in circles after the wayward piglets, the pair were sweaty and exhausted – they hadn't managed to catch a single one. Gaga tried his best to direct the two ginormous pigs,

who were much more interested in eating
the food that had been spilled from a feed
bin – knocked over by one of their over-eager
offspring – than racing round the yard!

Ace and Gaga were ready to give up,
with Gaga in a heap on the ground, when
Bear appeared out of nowhere, roaring with
laughter.

'HAHAHAHAHAHAHA . . .

you two! Hahahahaha . . . so funny . . .
to watch . . . hahahaha . . . I'm sorry, I'm
sorry . . . aha . . . but that was priceless.'

Ace was NOT impressed. 'You've been
watching the **WHOLE TIME?**' he
shrieked, still breathing heavily after his
farmyard workout.

Bear nodded and burst out laughing
again.

'Can you help us get them back in or
not?' Ace said, a lot grumpier than usual.

Still laughing, Bear picked up a bucket
from across the yard. She totally ignored
all the piglets and walked over to where
the two big pigs had stationed themselves
by the feed bin. She lifted the bin back

up and closed its lid. Then she started scooping the spilled food up from the ground until most of it was in the bucket. It still took a little bit of jostling and bucket-shaking, but eventually both the big pigs were back in their pen in the stables where they belonged – with a bit of extra food for their troubles.

A very smug Bear immediately closed the gate, even though the piglets were still out in the yard running riot. Ace watched in amazement as, one by one, the little pigs began to realize that Mum and Dad were no longer out and ran headlong, squealing, towards the stable door. The noise was deafening but Bear kept the pen closed for an extra second or two before opening it. It was mind-blowing! The piglets were practically begging to be let in and filed through the gate as quickly as they'd broken out of it!

Ace was still in shock when Bear introduced herself to Gaga, who had finally managed to dust himself off and stand upright again.

'Hi, I'm Bear. It's a real pleasure to meet you,' she said in the sweetest voice she could manage.

'Well, Bear, I'm Gaga. What a pleasure to meet you too! I can't believe how easily you did that! You'll have to excuse us – we're new to this kind of thing.'

Bear looked at Ace and giggled before saying, 'If you want, I can show you where to get food and supplies from? Follow me!'

13

Gaga parked his bike right in front of the door to Baverstock Country Supplies.

'*This way*,' sang Bear as she walked towards the store, saying 'good morning' to her fellow villagers. Gaga grabbed a trolley and followed her lead, exchanging 'good morning' greetings cheerily with everyone he saw.

Ace couldn't believe his eyes as he walked into the massive barn. There were big machines and small machines; there were hoppers and feeders and livestock houses; biscuits, treats and all sorts of snacks for every animal you could imagine – all in one place! His hands went wild, grabbing up as much as his arms could carry.

'Bear! Come and help me with this!' he shouted across the aisles.

The two of them ran up and down, depositing their findings in the trolley as Gaga stood chatting to someone he'd met wearing an Irish rugby shirt. Had he been paying attention, rather than trying to charm the whole village, he might have noticed Ace and Bear going a little overboard with their selection of goodies for the animals.

When they reached the queue for the

till, their trolley was full of pig food, cat food, vitamins and nutrients, paint, planks of wood, buckets and even a farm first-aid kit (one of the few items Gaga actually put in!) in case any of the animals fell ill. They had everything they needed and, as was customary when Ace visited any kind of shop with his Gaga, he was allowed to choose one thing for himself while they waited in the queue.

'You too, Bear,' Gaga said with a grin. She tried to decline as politely as she could, but Gaga was having none of it. 'It's tradition.'

Bear gave a 'thank you, that's very kind of you' smile and picked up a beanie hat with the same 'Eat, Sleep, Farm, Repeat'

slogan as Gaga had on his T-shirt.

Ace couldn't decide what he wanted. It was like he was in Aladdin's cave; it was so full of treasures. There were Bellevue snow globes on one wall and a complete range of magic watercolour booklets in every theme available on another, from superheroes to ballerinas and everything in between. There was a whole host of trinkets like kaleidoscopes and binoculars and, in the book section, there was an activity book that claimed to have 250 dot-to-dot pictures to be completed. How on earth was he supposed to make a decision?

He ran back to the till with the snow globe, binoculars and a 1,000-piece tractor puzzle because he just couldn't decide which he wanted the most. Gaga was loading up the last of the shopping – and that's when Ace saw them. There, right behind the cashier, was the brightest pair of yellow wellies.

'Sorry, Gaga,' Ace said, before turning to the cashier. 'Actually, can I leave these? I'd really like those yellow wellies behind you, please?'

The cashier smiled. 'Of course you can. Better check they're the right size first though!' she said, as she handed them over.

Size three. Perfect.

'Gaga, can I have these?' Ace said hopefully.

'Fine choice!' Gaga said.

They returned to the farmyard to find
Gigi busy in the workshop, wrench in
hand, putting the finishing touches to the
cherry picker she'd designed using the old
ride-on lawnmower cabin and a discarded
digger arm.

She shouted over to Ace, Gaga and Bear,
'How did you get on with the shopping?'

Ace started talking excitedly. 'We went
to the coolest farm-supply store, which
had *everything* you could imagine in it:
houses and beds and food and treats . . .'
he said. 'And then Gaga let us both get a
present each!'

'I got this hat and Ace got those wellies,'
added Bear.

Gigi laughed. 'Well, why don't you three
unpack everything and I can show you
what I've managed to create . . . I'm just
about done.'

★

'So, what's the plan, Ace?' Bear asked, as
they headed up to the house after they'd
put the farm supplies away.

'Well, I think we see what Gigi has managed to build and then we can take it from there. You reckon you can show me how to handle the animals like you did earlier?' said Ace, walking behind his new friend.

'Sure! It's easy enough,' said Bear.

Following her to the back door, Ace grabbed his new yellow wellies and put them on with a smile. He loved new shoes. They smelled delicious – like they'd been dunked in a barrel of fresh strawberries and left to soak before being sold.

As soon as Ace took his first steps back out into the fresh air, he noticed that his feet felt a little tingly and peculiar. He seemed to have more of a spring in his step and assumed that it was down to his shiny new wellies. It's funny how new shoes make you feel like you can run faster and jump higher, isn't it?

As he opened the farm gate, he watched Gaga jigging around to a song that was playing on the radio, humming to himself periodically while he set about the task of repainting the stables.

Bear was making her way towards the stable block when the strangest thing happened. The donkey, which had been braying while Ace was up in the house (as donkeys tend to do from time to time), very clearly said the words, 'Oh goodness gracious, pleeeease can somebody make it stop?'

The pigs and the goats, which were outside in temporary pens, began piping up too, but instead of squeals, grunts and bleats, Ace heard:

'Just you leave him alone, you grumpy old donkey,' said one goat.

'Ye-e-e-e-eah,' added the other. 'He can da-a-a-aaance if he wants to!'

'I actually quite like his moves,' said the smaller of the two big pigs, who'd made a point of brushing Gaga with her nose whenever he came close enough.

Ace couldn't believe his ears.

'NO WAY did a pig, two goats and a donkey just speak,' he muttered in confusion under his breath.

Almost immediately the smaller of the

two pigs diverted her attention from Gaga
to Ace.

'We've always spoken, young man,'
she replied. 'It's just that you humans can
never seem to understand us!'

Ace's face was a picture. His eyes
were wider than two full moons and his
mouth formed an 'O' large enough that
Gigi's motorcycle
could probably
have parked right
inside it!

Bear shouted over
to Ace from across
the yard. 'You all right
there, Ace? You look
a little funny!'

Ace managed to close his mouth in enough time to run over to where Bear was busily trying to break down the bales of hay into much lighter, more manageable piles.

'*Did . . . you . . . hear that?*' Ace whispered, suddenly becoming conscious of the other ears that might potentially be listening.

'Hear what?' Bear replied.

'The pig!' said Ace. 'It talked to me! With words. In English, not Pig!'

Bear looked at Ace warily. 'Is this some kind of joke? You're not trying to get back at me for laughing at you earlier, are you?'

'NO!' Ace said, turning back to the pig. She was looking straight at him. It was a

bit of an animal–human showdown, but
the pig broke rank first.

She definitely wasn't grunting when she
said, 'So what's your name then?'

'A-A-A-Ace,' he replied in an incredibly
shaky voice. He had tried to sound cool
and collected, but he'd failed miserably.
He looked over his shoulder, hoping that
Bear was close enough to lend her support,
but, of course, she'd disappeared again.
Meanwhile, the goats had begun frolicking
and bucking for joy at Ace's reply.

'Oh wow! He must be related to us – he
sounds just like we do!'

'Well, hello, Ace, welcome to our farm,'
said the pig. 'My name's Ginger. The
grumpy donkey is called Bumble! He's

actually rather nice when you get to know him.'

There was something incredibly reassuring about Ginger. Just those few words had already made Ace feel more relaxed than he'd felt all day, but his mind was still puzzling over just *how* he was able to understand her.

The goats were still in their pen next to Ginger and the other pig. One looked like it was in a trance, eating a piece of paper that had once been part of a bag of animal feed. Ginger just shook her head and chuckled as Ace spoke up.

'So who are these two?' he asked, pointing at the goats.

Ginger moved a little closer to the

gate where Ace was standing.

'These are the twins! Pickle's the boy and Pie's the girl!'

Right at that moment, one of Ginger's piglets ran out under the bars of the pen and started biting the toecaps of Ace's wellies.

Ace laughed at the tiny piglet, but he was horrified to see a dark-brown stain decorating his left foot. It was wet and runny and, worse still, the stench coming from it was far more disgusting than anything he'd ever smelled in the city.

'Oops!' Ginger giggled. 'I see you've already got acquainted with one of my munchkins. This handsome pig here is their father, Bruiser.'

Ginger's boar, who was almost twice the size of her, was armed with tusks that looked like they could rip through sheet metal in seconds. Ace had never thought of pigs as being scary before.

'Ooooh, Ace, delighted to meet you! I'm so glad you're here – you're just what we

need! And in case you were wondering –'
Bruiser's voice lowered to a whisper –
'apples are my absolute favourite!'

'Bruiser!' said Ginger, poking him
playfully with her nose.

Ace smiled. 'I'll try to remember that,
Bruiser.'

Looks can be deceiving, Ace thought. He
liked the big, friendly giant of a pig,
but the jury was still out on the piglets.
Ginger was trying to introduce Ace to her
children one by one, but they wouldn't
stand still long enough for her to get
through all their names. Ace threw caution
to the wind and stepped into the pen to
get a better look at the piglets, who were
busy exploring their surroundings.

'Sorry, which one's which?' he asked.

Before Ginger could reply, the piglets all began speaking at once.

'I'm Dexter, I'm the eldest . . .'

'Hey, I'm Duke, I'm the biggest boy . . .'

'Don't you worry about them – I'm Daisy, the cleverest of the piglets, thank you very much . . .'

'Yeah, yeah, yeah, name's Dakota, the coolest out of everyone, obviously, in case you didn't know . . .'

'Doug, nice to meet you – I get a bit nervous around people – sorry I pooed on your shoe . . .'

'Hey, Ace, I'm Diana. I'm the baby and I have Mummy and Daddy wrapped around my little piggy-toes!'

Ace felt more confused than ever.

'Sorry about that,' said Ginger. 'They get excited around new people. Their names are Dexter, Daisy, Doug, Diana, Dakota and Duke. I named them all with the letter D,' she said with pride, before adding, 'although, upon reflection, I *do* think that makes it slightly more difficult to remember who is who. Now, Ace, be a dear and let me out of this pen so I can introduce you to the other animals who live here.'

'Um . . . are you sure, Ginger? I really don't need a repeat of what happened last time,' Ace said hesitantly.

'Oh, don't worry, dear – you don't have to let us *all* out. Just me – leave this rabble in here.'

Here goes nothing, Ace thought to himself,
as he opened up the gate.

Quick as a flash, the big pig was out.

14

Ginger shot past Ace, as if eager to get a break from her overactive piglets. Then she began trotting across the yard and out of sight round the corner.

'Better get a move on,' Bruiser said to Ace. 'She's got a nifty set of feet on her!'

Ace ran after Ginger across the middle of the yard.

★

While all this was going on, Bear had been watching from the roof of the stables. She'd sneaked up on to it to get a bit of peace and quiet while working on a little gift for Ace: a map of the farm. She liked climbing on to the roof because no one else went up there, and she'd noticed that these days people almost always looked down and not up. Up there, she could watch everything without being noticed.

She had a lot to teach Ace about farm and country life, but she also knew he needed to learn much of it 'on the job'. She lived three houses down from Ace's farm with her mum and dad. Her parents ran a farm shop in the neighbouring village, so she was often left to her own devices. She'd always loved the look of Ace's uncle's farm and was glad that he'd let her look after his animals while he was away.

She was astonished at how quickly Ace seemed to have picked things up. She was even more blown away by the fact that Ginger was standing right next to him, as they both headed towards the chickens' enclosure. Having paused in her drawing, she thought it best to observe a little longer before announcing her presence again.

On his way to the chicken coop, Ace peered into the darkness of the hay barn and caught a glimpse of Gaga throwing hay around while dancing to a Bruno Mars song that was pumping out of the speakers. The barn was already much tidier than when he'd first laid eyes on it, so Ace continued round the corner to join Ginger.

'That's Charlie. He's the finest cockerel in Bellevue and he's got the loudest call for miles too!' she said.

'Oh, don't I know it,' replied Ace. 'I've never heard anything like it in my life!'

Ginger chuckled. 'Yes, it gave the piglets quite a fright the first time they heard it too. Poor things. It does take some getting used to.'

Ace opened the enclosure and, at once, Charlie came strutting over.

'How-d'you-dooooo?' he said in his cool sing-songy style.

Ace was thankful it was much quieter than the morning call.

'I'm feeling a bit better now that I've actually met some of you, thank you.

I'm Ace – pleased to meet you.'

There was a flurry of activity coming from inside the coop and, all of a sudden, Ace could hear the muffled voices of three hens getting louder and louder as they walked outside to where he was standing.

The cockerel cleared his throat and announced: 'A-a-ace, meet Agatha, Pixie and Floss, the str–, er, ch-chickens of, er, this fine coop.'

Charlie had wanted to say 'the stroppy chickens' but, as he valued his life, he thought better of it.

Ginger nuzzled as close to Ace's ear as she could. 'Agatha's top of the pecking order. If anything needs pecking, it's her that gets to do it first.'

Ace didn't reply, but he nodded in understanding.

Agatha was white all over, with a black ring of feathers just above her neck. She was the plumpest of the hens when in full feather, and she had a bright red comb and wattle, which contrasted beautifully with her white body. Ace watched her in amazement.

As he leaned back into Ginger, he asked, 'How comes she's so big?'

BIG MISTAKE.

'**Big?! BIG?!** Who you calling *big*?' replied Agatha, full of fury, and she immediately started flapping her wings and strutting after the other two hens.

Thankfully, she'd not realized the
question had come from Ace, otherwise
she might have chased him right out of
the enclosure!

'Shhh-shhh-shhhh!' replied Ginger.
'Make sure you whisper. Agatha has a
mean old streak! In any case, she's the top
hen – what they call the alpha – so *that's*

why she's the biggest. Plus, she'll never admit it, but she's probably eaten more than her fair share of food!'

Ginger and Ace shared a chuckle, then went back to watching the chickens.

'Who's the black hen over there?' Ace said in a whisper.

'Well, now, that's Pixie,' replied Ginger. 'She's actually blue, not black, but she's certainly the prettiest with all those dark feathers of hers. Loves to preen herself, that one.'

Pixie's comb and wattle were a lovely, mellow shade of pink.

Gaga would most definitely approve, thought Ace.

At that moment, Agatha accidentally

stepped on Pixie's left wing.

'WATCH WHERE YOU'RE STRUTTING, you old bird!' she said to Agatha.

Ace was about to open his mouth to introduce himself when Floss, the third hen, piped up.

'Oh, put a cob in it, Pixie, you prancing, preening princess! If you did more than just primp those feathers of yours, maybe she wouldn't have stepped on them in the first place!'

'And that's Floss,' said Ginger with a sigh. 'As you can see, she's the smallest of the chickens and – if you can believe it – the snappiest.'

Ace arched his eyebrows in appreciation,

afraid to say anything out of turn.

'She's what they call a hybrid: a little bit of this and a little bit of that, all mixed up into one fiery ball of chicken. She's also *very* house-proud.'

Floss announced that she was making her exit. 'I've had enough of the pair of you. I'm off to **BED!**'

And, with that, she turned and strutted off with her head held high.

Ace grinned. Those hens were definitely going to be hard work.

★

Ginger continued to be Ace's guide around the farm. She took him up past the field where Sybil the cow was chewing grass. As Ace watched her chew, he saw the black cat walking along the fence in the distance.

'*Who's the cat, Ginger?*' Ace whispered.

'That's Phantom. He's a funny one. Pretends he wants to be all by himself but he's almost always hiding somewhere close by.'

Ace went towards Phantom to say hi and introduce himself, but, as soon as the cat caught sight of him, Phantom dashed away, running back towards the farmhouse.

As Ace and Ginger made their way back to the farmyard, his mind wandered back to his meeting with Councillor Crabbington and an idea suddenly popped into his head.

It was a brave notion to gather all the animals out of their pens after the pandemonium of the morning, but that's what Ace did that afternoon, while they were all enjoying their naps.

'Up you get, everyone!' said Ace, clanging a pot with a wooden spoon. 'If you could all line up nicely in front of your pens, that would be fantastic!'

The animals were quite unused to being woken up in this fashion.

As Ace walked through the yard, he could see how much work had been done in just one day. The hay barn was looking spotless, and Gigi had made great progress in fixing the broken machinery. She and Gaga were just closing up the workshop area as Bear emerged from the barn and greeted Ace. For the first time in forever, Bear was lost for words as her jaw dropped open in astonishment at the sight before her.

Ace was holding Sybil's halter, walking peacefully through the gate with Ginger and all six piglets closely following behind.

'My goodness, Ace! This is incredible! How on earth did you get those pigs to do that?' marvelled Gaga.

Ace smiled as he passed him, deciding to keep hold of his secret for a little while longer.

'There you are, Ace! I wondered where you'd got to,' said Gigi, before adding, 'Oh my **WORD!**' as Ace very calmly and expertly lined up each group of animals side by side.

'Look, everyone, I brought us all together today because I wanted you to know that we're a team and we can get the farm up to scratch in no time.'

Both grandparents and Bear looked on in wonder. Not only was Ace addressing the animals as if he were a head teacher, but what happened next was even stranger, because Ace's words were met with a chorus of moos and brays and grunts and clucks!

Ace's day may have started off badly, but things were definitely looking up.

15

You have probably already gathered that Councillor Henry Crabbington was not a particularly nice man.

You might be wondering why people voted for such a person to be their councillor. The truth was that Councillor Crabbington hadn't always been 'Crabby' Crabbington. Thirty years ago, he'd simply been 'Happy Henry' to all the local villagers. As a young man, he was known for being helpful, kind and putting other people's needs before his own.

He won the local election to become councillor by a landslide and the villagers were happy with their choice. The newly appointed Councillor Crabbington made sure the village was well looked after, that small businesses were supported, that the villagers could come to him with any problems and he'd always do his best to help them. The villagers loved Henry so much that they voted for him to remain their councillor for the rest of his life! That was ten years ago and, not long after, everything changed.

It was the night of the village fire. Young Councillor Crabbington had just locked up the village hall after a brilliant day's work. Bellevue had been voted Britain's most beautiful village and it was almost all thanks to him . . . and the villagers, of course! Every unruly hedge had been hacked, every overgrown shrub had been scrubbed, and every street corner in the village rendered so spotless you could eat your Sunday roast right off the pavement – gravy and all.

Lucky me! Crabbington said to himself, closing the door to his two-bedroom flat at the top of the village-hall building. Tonight, Henry Crabbington the Third was celebrating! He was going all out and making creamy spinach-stuffed salmon in garlic butter with all the trimmings; it was his – and his childhood sweetheart, Violet's – favourite meal.

Dusk was just beginning to fall when he heard what sounded like a series of little pops coming from the back garden. It was a strange sound, but a quick look outside, coupled with the fact that nothing out of the ordinary ever really happened in Bellevue, left Crabbington comfortable enough to carry on with his plans for the evening.

I need a great bottle of wine tonight. The best money can buy! OK, maybe not that much but a great bottle nonetheless! thought Henry.

He gave Violet a quick call to confirm the details for dinner.

'Hello, you . . . Yes, yes, it's been a delightful day! Thank you . . . OK . . . Yes, see you at six at mine and don't forget to bring the cheese knives! Bye!'

With a spring in his step, Councillor
Crabbington went out and popped into
Delvey's Wine Merchants. Then, armed
with a bottle of pink champagne that was
impossible to pronounce, he walked a few
doors down to Rob and Dara Birchfield's
garden centre.

'Hey up, Crabbington! What can I do

you for?' Rob asked cheerily.

'Well, actually, I was wondering if your lovely wife, Dara, would be able to make up a bouquet of flowers for Violet.'

'Just take yourself on down there, past the orchids, and you'll see her in the flower hut. It's nearly time for closing but I'm sure she'll work something out for you,' said Rob.

And she did.

'There you go, pet,' said Dara, producing a bountiful bouquet of lilies, as pink as the champagne Henry had tucked under his arm.

'No charge, Councillor, and congratulations again on the beautiful village award,' she said, smiling at him.

Henry took a deep sniff of the flowers. 'Thank you, Dara – you're far too kind.'

How wonderful it is when you get things for free! thought Henry, as he strutted across the road to his last stop: Del and Pat Norman's fishmonger's. It really was going to be the best evening ever.

The Normans owned the village butcher's, fishmonger's and the restaurant, Norman's Nosh. It was the most popular place to eat in the village, adjoining the fishmonger's, and Councillor Crabbington greeted both of them as the bell rang above the fishmonger's shop door.

'Hi, Del! Hello, Pat! I'd like two of your most succulent salmon fillets, please!' sang the councillor.

'Oooh, sounds like someone is pushing the boat out tonight! Has our little award win got anything to do with it?' replied Del, deliberately waving his towel across the Most Beautiful British Village award that was on the mantelpiece behind his counter. Henry had decided to let each of the shop owners keep the award for a month so that everyone could appreciate it.

The phone rang as Pat smiled up at the councillor.

'It looks good up there, don't you think? Thanks for letting us have it first,' she said.

She picked the fillets up from the weighing scales, wrapped them expertly in brown paper and popped them into a bag that said **NORMAN'S** underneath the shop logo.

'You're so very welcome,' replied Henry with a nod and a wink. 'Have a good evening!'

As he walked out of the shop, he bumped straight into a group of three teenagers he didn't recognize.

'Weirdo!' one said.

'Come on – keep up!' said another, as they all ran off, giggling, down the street.

Henry saw one of them throw something on the ground, which exploded with a small bang.

'No littering in the village!' he shouted after them. He picked up the discarded rubbish and was strolling back to his flat when two things happened at once.

Firstly, the smell of the lilies was

replaced with the smell of smoke. Confusion began to fill his brain as he tried to work out why there should be a smell of smoke so close to the high street. Just as he was thinking, *I hope the Normans' kitchen isn't on fire*, Del Norman came running out of the restaurant, yelling, **'FIRE!** At the village hall! **Quick!'**

Henry Crabbington ran towards the building that held his private and professional life within its walls.

'Nooooooo . . . !'

He screamed in distress as he saw the building enveloped in flames. Del Norman had to stop him from trying to get inside. Del held Henry as he cried and cried and cried.

When the fire had been brought under control, a firefighter approached Henry. 'Unfortunately we believe the source of the fire to be a naked flame of some sort, which probably caught hold on the carpet in the flat upstairs. One of the windows was slightly ajar.'

Henry's heart sank. He had left the lounge window open – he always did when the weather was good.

But I don't have anything with a naked flame, he thought.

Then the penny dropped.

'Oh NO,' he said, as the millionth piece of his shattered heart divided again to make a million and one.

Those pops I heard on the street outside

Norman's were the same ones I heard in the garden before I left . . . It couldn't be!

There was no proof, but he was sure it had to be those terrible teens playing with fireworks and they'd been using the wall of *his* flat as target practice.

By the time Violet had arrived and heard everything that had happened, Councillor Crabbington's sadness had been replaced with an anger that burned hot enough to roast marshmallows on.

'Henry,' she pleaded, 'it's OK. Just talk to me. Everything is insured and we'll work this all out.'

But Henry couldn't be consoled. He flew off in his car, filled with rage and resentment, and crashed it into the

Rotten Reservoir. With no home and no car, Happy Henry was gone forever. He stopped greeting the villagers and he distrusted every young person he met.

'Where did looking after everyone else get me? It's time I looked after number one,' he said to himself.

★

Since that night, Crabbington's only aim had been to get back everything he had lost – with interest – and abusing his power as a councillor gave him a way to do just that. He had the final say on local laws being passed and, in particular, Henry Crabbington took great care to learn all the tricks to obtaining ownership of village property.

First Fruits Farm was one of the few buildings left in Bellevue that Councillor Crabbington didn't own. He'd been working on a plan to obtain the farm for himself ever since he'd discovered that Hakim Akbar hadn't been living there and the property was becoming more and more neglected. He wasn't actually interested in keeping it as a farm – it was a large property in a great location. His plan was to get his hands on it and sell it to the property developer who offered the most money. They could turn it into flats or a shopping centre or a rubbish dump for all he cared.

He'd very recently passed a law that allowed any land in the village to be sold if it had been in disrepair for thirty days or longer. He knew that if the farm had an inspection in its current state, it would most certainly fail and have to be sold to the highest bidder – in other words, him!

What he hadn't prepared for was Ace, Gaga, Gigi and Bear.

16

Ace was up early on Monday for his first day at Bellevue Primary School. He was pretty nervous and couldn't even eat the delicious breakfast Gigi had prepared.

Ace's nerves increased as Gaga rolled up outside the school gates on the Harley-Davidson. Both Gaga and Ace were wearing helmets and leather jackets, and the group of kids standing outside the gate had all stopped talking and were staring at Ace and the motorbike as if they were aliens from outer space.

Ace climbed out, said goodbye to Gaga and, for the first time in his life, really felt like an outsider. Gaga certainly looked like one, wearing a pair of canary-yellow chinos and a petrol-blue shirt.

'Fancy turning up to school on a motorbike!'

The voice belonged to Oscar Norman, Bellevue Primary School's head boy and son of Del and Pat Norman. Oscar

stood next to Isabel Birchfield and Alfie McMillan, who joined him in sniggering at Ace's method of transport to school.

'Nice jacket,' Isabel sneered, 'but you won't be needing that in school. Should have worn a pair of wellies, really – this is the countryside, you know.'

Rats. Ace had been so nervous about his first day at school that he had forgotten to pack his wellies. He looked around and every child was wearing school uniform, complete with wellington boots. Ace wished the ground would swallow him whole.

'Morning, Ace! Come with me – I'll show you where everything is,' Bear said.

Feeling very relieved, Ace followed her

away from the crowd of gawking kids and into the school. As she hung up her book bag in the cloakroom, she turned to Ace.

'Right, ready for some school rules?' Before waiting for him to reply, she began. 'Rule number one: stick with me and you'll be just fine. Rule number two: bring a packed lunch to school because we can use our break times to work on our farm plans. Rule number three –' she looked down at his feet – 'never, **EVER** forget your wellies. Got it?'

'Yep, got it,' Ace replied. 'Where do I sit?'

'Right next to me,' said Bear, which instantly made Ace's day so much better.

★

In the end, it wasn't the worst day ever.

Ace kept himself to himself during his lessons and spent every break time with Bear, sketching out what still needed doing on the farm to get it ready for the inspection. Lots of the lessons involved them spending time outside, so Ace soon realized why rule number three was 'never, **EVER** forget your wellies'. But it wasn't until his science lesson in the afternoon that he realized just how extraordinary *his* wellies were.

Ace and Bear had been placed in a working group of five with Isabel, Oscar and Alfie. The school had their own flock of sheep, which belonged to Mr Baker, their teacher, and that term they were learning all about the characteristics of sheep. Ace hadn't worked with sheep before – in fact, he knew nothing about them – and Isabel, Alfie and Oscar picked up on it very quickly.

'We've heard all about your farm, you know, but I bet it's not a *real* farm like mine!' said Alfie.

'Of course it is,' replied Ace. 'We might not have sheep, but we have lots of other animals!'

'Well, from what we can see, you have no idea what you're doing, do you?' said Isabel.

Ace didn't want to admit it, but it was true. Even worse, he couldn't work out why he was unable to communicate with these sheep like he could with his own animals. His mind went back to something Ginger had said that day: 'We've always spoken,' she'd said. So why couldn't he hear the sheep and understand them now? Every time he went to touch one of them, they responded with a firm **'baaa'** and ran off.

Alfie laughed out loud, saying, 'See, no clue. I've been to your farm before and I've never seen a more random set of animals.'

'Don't you worry about them. They're **OUR** animals and none of your business,' said Bear, returning from the loo and joining the conversation.

'Exactly,' said Ace, who was angry at Alfie for calling his animals 'random'.

They might well have been random, but they were *his* Farm Squad. Well, his, Gaga, Gigi and Bear's, and they all loved them, which was enough.

'We've heard about your inspection ... No chance you're gonna pass that if you carry on like this,' said Oscar.

'How do you know about that?' said Ace, perplexed.

'Let's just say we know people in high places and there's nothing we don't hear about in this village,' Oscar replied with a slice of malice in his voice.

Before Ace could argue back, the bell rang and Mr Baker dismissed everyone for the day.

Ace was relieved to see the trio run off towards the classroom and he hung back with Bear to pick her brains.

'Bear, I don't know what just happened there, but I literally couldn't handle those sheep at all!' he said.

'Yeah, what was up with that?' Bear replied. 'I've seen how you handled

Ginger and that was like night and day compared to what you were like with those sheep.'

'I've no idea,' said Ace, as he and Bear made for the school gates.

'Well, I don't have to be home until six tonight so I can come with you to the farm and we can try handling the animals again if you like?' Bear offered.

Ace and Bear both squished into Gaga's sidecar and made the journey back to First Fruits Farm. Ace was impatient to see the animals and, as his shoes were already muddy because he'd forgotten his wellies that day, he asked Gaga to drop the two of them off at the farm instead of up at the house.

At the side gate, they scrambled out and went to see Gigi in her workshop.

'Hi, Gigi – how's your day been?' said Ace.

Gigi stopped drilling a piece of metal and looked up at the two of them with a smile. She dusted down her charcoal-grey, fireproof apron and lifted up her welding mask, which made her look more like a robot than a human. Her pink, orange and yellow floral-print trainers made her feet stand out among all the dark protective clothing.

'Oh, I've been very busy today! Come and have a look at what I've done.'

Gigi had been busy indeed, and exceptionally inventive as always.

'Remember you said you wanted me
to fix the farm up a bit? Well, I went one
better. These will make sure that there's no
other farm in the world like it. See!'

Ace and Bear's eyes opened wide in
amazement. Right in front of them were
the most elaborate plans for the farm.

'These are just my first ideas, but when it's finished it'll be incredible, trust me,' Gigi added proudly.

'Oh wow!' said Bear. 'This is like the most incredible science experiment I've ever seen.'

'If you think this is great, wait till I show you how it all works,' said Gigi. 'I know how much you love the animals, so we're going to get Gaga to redesign the stables and pens to make them super comfy.'

Gigi was in her element, explaining all the drawings she'd carefully crafted that day.

'This is what the chicken coop will look like,' she continued. 'I've called it the

Strut Suite, fitted with its own individual pods for Agatha, Pixie and Floss to lay their eggs in peace.'

'**Whooooa!** How cool,' said Ace and Bear in unison.

'Precisely,' said Gigi. 'Plus, it allows Charlie the freedom to do his "cock-a-doodle-doo"ing without disturbing us too much!'

It was spectacular, to say the least, but Gigi wasn't finished.

'The key word for any top-of-the-range farm should be "sustainable". So I'm going to put solar panels on all the buildings to generate our own electricity, which in turn will power the buildings and machinery without any extra cost.

In fact, if we can generate enough power through the sun and the wind, we might even be able to sell some power back to the village to help keep a few of their services running!'

'That sounds brilliant!' said Bear. 'We've been learning about sustainability at school.'

'And so you should,' replied Gigi. 'It's really important that we think about resources that we can reuse. For energy, it means using techniques to locate and generate power from natural sources that won't run out.'

Bear nodded enthusiastically.

'And this,' continued Gigi, 'is my masterpiece, the centre point of the farm –

a humungous, interactive weathervane, which incorporates all sorts of weather-measuring instruments. I'll synchronize all their readings to my computer and they should be able to give us accurate four-weekly reports on the weather so that we can plan everything in advance! What do you think?'

Bear had been studying the plans intently and listening to everything being said. She had an idea.

'Ace, why don't we go and feed the animals and think about what *they* might want on the farm too.'

'Great point, Bear,' said Ace. 'But I can do even better than that: we'll just ask them outright! Gigi, we'll leave you to it.

Bear, let's go and speak to the animals!'

Bear had no idea what Ace was talking about, but she didn't want to burst his bubble now that he'd cheered up a bit. The two of them left Gigi to get back to her drilling and planning and went straight round to the stables where

Bumble, Pickle, Pie, Ginger, Bruiser and the piglets were all lounging about.

'OK, watch this,' Ace said to Bear as he headed towards Ginger. 'Right, animals, we need to save the farm from Councillor Crabbington, but I also want the farm to be the perfect place for you all to live. Tell me what changes you'd like to see.'

Instead of the hellos and answers he was expecting, all he could hear were grunts and Bumble's loud braying. He didn't understand: yesterday, he'd spoken to all the animals individually and he certainly hadn't been dreaming when he'd heard them speaking to him.

Ginger nodded her head and

started to speak again. But all Ace could hear were her grunts.

'I don't get it,' he said, turning to Bear, puzzled. 'Yesterday, I could hear them speaking perfectly – today, nothing.'

Bear did not look impressed. 'Ha. Ha. Look, Ace, I like a good joke as much as the next person but this whole "talking to the animals" stuff has got to stop. The only way to understand animals is to spend time with them.' She rolled her eyes. 'You've not even been here a week and the fresh air is already getting to you!'

At that moment, Doug, the piglet who'd pooed on Ace's shoe, ran out under the bars of the pig pen and straight over to Ace. He started nipping at Ace's toes,

making him look down. It was then
that he realized what was different from
yesterday.

Ace looked at Bear with a grin. Bear
looked at Ace, puzzled. As she watched
him turn and run towards the house, she
shouted, 'What are you doing now?!'

★

Quick as a flash, Ace ran up to the house,
through the back door and into the
kitchen, where the boots were resting
on their rack. He kicked off his
muddy school
shoes and
jumped into
the wellies.
The peculiar

tingly feeling came rushing back and the spring in his step returned. Even quicker than a flash, Ace was through the back door and in the farmyard, standing next to Bear. She had her arms tightly crossed over her chest, waiting impatiently for Ace.

'Go on then – let's see you perform your miracle,' said Bear.

Ace took a deep breath and said to the animals, 'OK, Farm Squad, let's try this again. Ginger, what do you think we should do here on the farm to make it somewhere that you would love to live?'

And this time . . . it worked! All the piglets erupted in cheers and shouts, saying, 'Yay, we can hear him again!'

Ginger very calmly said, 'Well, dear,

those wellies are more than a little bit special, aren't they? If I were you, I wouldn't let them out of your sight! Now, to answer your question, I've always dreamed of having my own woodland and wallow, so that we can take dips in the summer and these pesky piglets of mine will stop running off and getting lost in the woods by the orchard. It will be like one big adventure playground on their doorstep.'

Bear could still only hear a collection of animal noises, but her expression had changed now that she could see the animals responding to Ace. She kept looking over to him, expecting to be updated at any moment. When nothing came, she tapped him on the shoulder.

'Er, hello, Ace? I'm still standing here! Did it work or what?'

Ace laughed. He'd forgotten that Bear wasn't able to hear what he was hearing. He decided there and then that he needed to try to get some magic yellow wellies for Bear too.

'Yes, it worked!' he told her.

'Prove it,' replied Bear.

'OK,' said Ace. 'Tell me something you want the animals to do and I'll get them to do it.'

Still unsure of whether to believe Ace or not, Bear tried to think of something so complicated that there'd be no doubt she had asked it.

'Tell the goats to run over to the water trough, jump over it five times each and then climb on to each other's backs.'

It was obvious that Bear didn't believe the animals could do any of that, but she was about to be proved wrong.

She watched smugly as Ace said to the goats, 'Pickle, Pie, can the two of you run over to the water trough and jump over it five times? Then, Pie, you jump on Pickle's back.'

In two shakes of a goat's tail, the twins followed the instructions perfectly. Bear was stunned into silence, her bottom jaw almost hitting the ground.

'Now do you believe me?' Ace asked, a grin dancing across his lips.

'That was **AWESOME!**' said Bear, clapping her hands in excitement.

★

After the animals were fed, Ace asked each of them what changes they would like to see on the farm, while Bear wrote their responses down on paper.

'OK, this is what we have so far,' Bear said. 'Bumble said he feels quite lonely at times and could do with being able to see everyone else in the stables – especially at night. Pickle, Pie and Sybil all agreed on some outdoor space with direct access to the stables for bedtimes.

'Sybil asked for fresh vegetables in her daily meals. Oh, and a mineral lick. I know they do those at Baverstock. They're kind of like ice lollies for animals – horses in particular *love* them, so it should be simple enough to add on to our next shopping list.'

WHAT THE ANIMALS WANT

- Ginger, Bruiser and the piglets: own woodland (safe place to run around) and wallow pit
- Bumble: wants to be able to see everyone else
- Pickle, Pie and Sybil: outdoor space with direct access to stables for bedtimes
- Sybil: fresh vegetables and a mineral lick

Ace and Bear nodded to each other, happy with their work.

'Let's go and show Gaga,' said Ace.

★

'Excellent notes,' Gaga confirmed, 'and excellent ideas! It's almost as if the animals told you what they needed themselves! This weekend I'll make sure we get all the necessary bits so that we can press ahead!'

Gigi had finished up her work for the day, so Ace proudly presented the list to her as well.

'Oh, Ace, this is fantastic. When all this is done, we'll pass that inspection with flying colours! There's lots of work to be done but, for now, dinner! I've made a lovely chicken soup – Bear, would you like to stay for . . . ? Oh! Where's she gone?' said Gigi.

'Bear? Beeeeaaaaar!' shouted Ace after his friend. He shook his head, slightly miffed that she'd vanished into thin air without saying goodbye. 'She's done it again! That girl would make a great magician; she's an expert at disappearing unannounced. Oh well, more chicken soup for me! Last one in the house is a rotten egg . . . !'

17

Henry Crabbington was in a foul mood. Today was *not* going to plan. To start with, his alarm clock hadn't gone off so he was late for work. There was no cereal left for his breakfast, the fruit in his smoothie was rotten and his only clean pair of socks was full of holes. It was catastrophe after catastrophe.

By the time he arrived at the village hall, he was over an hour late. Since meeting Ace, Councillor Crabbington's mind had been primarily preoccupied with formulating a plan to take over First Fruits Farm. He wondered whether it might be time to pay another visit – to check on their progress, or lack thereof. He hunched over his desk, pressing his knuckles into the desktop.

'Oliver!' he shouted to his long-suffering personal assistant, Oliver Pink – the only person who had really stuck by him during those dark days after he'd lost everything.

'Y-yes, Mr Crabbington,' came the flustered reply.

'Get me the minutes from the last village council meeting and the list of attendees for the upcoming one.'

Oliver hesitated a moment.

'Well, what are you waiting for? Do it **NOW!**' shouted the councillor.

Oliver Pink was the only person in the village who was able to tolerate Crabbington for any length of time, perhaps because he had been born without a sense of smell and perhaps because, despite Crabbington's meanness,

Oliver believed that deep down there was still kindness in him.

He ran into Crabbington's office and handed him the papers, which were still warm from being freshly printed. In his haste, he dropped them all over the desk and on to the floor.

'Oh my, I'm so, so, SO sorry! I'll tidy that up right away!' he said.

'Don't bother,' spat Crabbington with real venom in his voice. 'I'll do it myself! Go and make me a cup of tea, if that's not too difficult!'

He waved Oliver away dismissively.

Henry studied the papers intently and looked at the agenda items for the next council meeting.

> • Approval of renovation plans for First Fruits Farm

A wicked smile curled on his lips. He'd just had a very cunning idea.

★

The week flew by as Ace settled into his new routine. Gaga took him to school as Gigi worked on the plans for the farm renovation. Bear and Ace were inseparable and spent their break times coming up with ways to improve the farm plans.

Two weeks before the inspection, Gigi

and Gaga asked both children to meet them in the kitchen.

'So this is it,' Gigi began. 'The final plans will be submitted to the council tomorrow afternoon.'

Ace and Bear watched in wonder as both their and the animals' dreams were unfolded on the piece of paper in front of them.

'Gigi, it's ... **brilliant**,' said Ace in amazement.

'I thought you might say that,' said Gigi, pleased with herself and her work. 'It still has to stand up to the test of the council, but I'd hope such an innovative design would never be rejected.'

The smile on Bear's face was replaced

with a furrow in her brow.

'If that meeting is anything like meetings I've been to with Mum and Dad before, you'd better believe Councillor Crabbington will have his own agenda. He'll do everything he can to get these plans thrown out,' she said.

'You're probably right,' Ace said in return, 'but all we can do is try.'

Bear grinned. 'If anyone can do it, the Farm Squad certainly can!'

18

It was the evening of the council meeting and Ace hadn't touched a morsel of food on his plate. Gigi had left him and Bear a huge lasagne to warm up with a delicious Caribbean coleslaw made with red cabbage and raisins. Usually it would be gone in a minute but today they'd hardly eaten a thing.

Bear threw down her fork, looking fed up. 'That's it. I can't stay here all night wondering what's happening in that meeting. Let's go.'

Clutching a piece of garlic bread, Bear marched out of the door, with Ace running to catch her up.

★

At 6 p.m. on the dot, Councillor Crabbington called the Bellevue council meeting to order and addressed its attendees.

'The purpose of the meeting tonight is to discuss the renovation plans for First Fruits Farm. I am pleased to introduce Daniel O'Sullivan and Carmen George as its new owners and to welcome them to our wonderful village.'

Gaga and Gigi both stood and gave a wave.

'Thank you for that kind welcome,' Gaga said, 'but the farm actually belongs to our grandson, Ace Sinclair.'

There was a ripple of soft clapping around the room, to welcome them, before Crabbington continued: 'I trust you all received a copy of the plans, so I open up the floor for discussion before we take a vote for approval.'

Councillor Crabbington sat back down in his seat, which looked more like a throne with its purple velvet upholstery and gilt frame.

★

Bear and Ace had run over to the village hall where the council meeting was being held. Before they reached the front door, Bear ducked into an alley down the side of it. Halfway along the alley, there was a wooden door with a frosted glass window. Bear went up to it and with one swift movement pushed the door open. Ace stared in astonishment.

'How did you do that? How did you know it would be open?' he said.

'This is the countryside; nobody locks

anything. Now stop stalling and get in here, otherwise we'll miss all the juicy bits of the meeting!'

Ace and Bear raced up the staircase into a gallery area that overlooked the hall. They could see Gaga and Gigi, and Councillor Crabbington sitting on his ridiculous throne. They were just in time.

★

It was Del Norman, the owner of Norman's Nosh, who spoke first.

'I have to admit, I've never seen any plans like it. Gonna be pretty state of the art when it's finished, isn't it? Probably just the thing we need here in the village,' he said.

Pat Norman, Del's wife, added in her

two pennies' worth as well. 'Well done, you two!'

Gaga and Gigi both smiled. This was a good start, especially considering that they didn't really know anybody in the village yet and they were a little nervous at how they would be received.

The Birchfields, owners of the village garden centre, followed the Normans' lead.

'Well, I agree. I think the plans are splendid,' said Dara, and Rob Birchfield nodded vigorously next to her.

Councillor Crabbington took charge of the meeting once again: 'All those in favour of passing the plans, raise your hand.'

Crabbington raised his hand to

demonstrate, then swiftly dropped it. However, the room was a sea of village hands and excitement began to build inside Gigi and Gaga.

'And all those against . . .'

Again, Crabbington raised his hand but, instead of dropping it, this time left it in the air.

'Ah, it would seem that the plans are to be approved . . .' he said, giving rise to another ripple of soft applause and hugs exchanged between Gaga and Gigi.

★

Up in the gallery, Ace nearly shouted out loud! Anticipating his excitement, Bear clapped her hand across his mouth just in time to stifle the noise.

'*SHHHHHHHH! You'll give our position away!*' Bear whispered sternly.

'*Sorry, sorry,*' Ace whispered back. '*I just can't believe it was that easy.*'

Bear raised an eyebrow – she wasn't convinced.

'*Keep watching. QUIETLY! Remember what I told you about Crabbington . . . He'll think of something to sabotage the plans.*'

★

She was right. Councillor Crabbington was not done. He paused briefly and shot a glance at the gallery seats, thinking he'd heard a noise. Satisfied that there was nothing to be concerned about, he continued speaking:

'Unfortunately there are a few, er, *technical* issues. Firstly, this property has Site of Special Scientific Interest status because there is a rare kind of flower growing on the farmland. This means that the plans need approval from the district board . . .'

The celebrations in the room gave way to horrified expressions. Turning to Gaga and Gigi, Crabbington continued.

'Such approval could take weeks, so

you'll have to be . . . er . . . patient.'

'Weeks!' groaned Ace from his hidden spot on the balcony. They only had two weeks left before the inspection!

But Crabbington still wasn't finished.

'Ah, did I forget to mention that First Fruits Farm also has an underground gas pipeline running through it? Fencing of any kind *must* have approval from the gas network. That will probably take a bit of time to organize as well.'

A ghastly grin stretched across his face as he looked at the villagers.

Ace stared down at them all in disbelief. Bear shook her head in frustration.

'Told you so,' she said with a sigh.

★

The room was deathly silent. This was how the council meetings had been going for a long time. The villagers came with ideas and the councillor found a loophole to get those ideas thrown out.

'Well, unless there is anything else, I think the meeting is over. I would be delighted if you would all stay and join me in a little light refreshment! Oliver, get the chocolate Hobnobs out – it's been a good meeting, I believe!'

Gaga and Gigi definitely didn't agree that it had been a good meeting, but they didn't want to lose hope yet.

'OK,' said Gigi, 'this isn't all bad. Ace won't be happy, but if we move quickly we might still be able to pull this off. You can put in calls to the relevant boards in the morning. Although it will be a Saturday, we should get replies by the end of the day on Monday. We might even get lucky with the gas network, as they'll have emergency teams working round the clock every day of the week.'

'Agreed,' said Gaga, munching on a Rich Tea biscuit. 'We know we have to wait for the fencing, but we can still build the animal accommodation and sort out the barn and stables, and you can develop the tools we'll need for everyday work.'

Gigi smiled. 'We won't be defeated that easily! No matter what the councillor says!'

Gaga nodded before adding, 'Anyway, let's meet some of our fellow villagers before we get back and break the news to Ace and Bear.'

Over their cups of tea, Gaga and Gigi got to know the Birchfields and the Normans. They even made a promise to visit Norman's Nosh for lunch the next day – after they'd got all the supplies they needed from Baverstock.

It was 7.15 p.m. when Councillor Crabbington rather unceremoniously began jangling his keys to get everyone to leave.

'All right, all right, time's up – let's get going!' he said, hustling everybody out of the room. 'Buh-bye, Del, lovely seeing you,' he said, hiding behind a fake smile he had perfected over the years. It disappeared as soon as the door was closed. He double-locked it, dusted off his hands and marched towards the back, shouting,

'Oliveeeeeeeer!'

★

Back at the farmhouse, Gaga and Gigi were filling Ace and Bear in on the meeting. They both pretended to be shocked by the news.

'**Grrrr**, that Councillor Crabbington is a piece of work! He could have told us that we needed to seek approval elsewhere first!' Ace said in frustration.

'Don't worry, Ace – remember what I told you,' said Bear. 'If you want to beat him, you have to be *smarter* than him. The question is *how*?'

'I know exactly how,' said Ace. 'We're going to start work tomorrow, as planned. Gaga, you're going to call all the boards to get that approval. With any luck, we'll get everything pushed through much quicker with your charm! Gigi, you keep working on those plans for the new farm machines, and Bear and I will see to the animals. We've come too far to give up now.'

19

Saturday was always pancake day. Gigi was going all out on the menu that morning, which featured blueberry-and-banana pancakes, maple-cured streaky bacon, avocados and farm-fresh poached eggs. She'd also prepared a homemade assortment of condiments: apricot marmalade, raspberry jam and honey.

Ace smiled as he peeked into the kitchen. He tiptoed through the door and tried to sneak a piece of bacon off the hotplate, but Gigi caught him in the act.

'Morning, Gigi,' he said, laughing, as she knocked his hand away. 'Where's Gaga?'

'Good morning to you too, Ace,' said Gigi brightly. 'He's been on the phone since eight. Go and see how he's getting on – breakfast will be ready in a minute.'

Ace left Gigi to work her magic and walked through the hallway and into the living room, which was now filled with their furniture. There, he spotted Gaga spinning round in his office chair, phone in hand, getting more and more tangled up in the phone cord as the sound of Gaga's laughter bounced round the room.

'Hahahahaha, I don't believe you – they used to be the *best* in all of Ireland and we *both* played there! Oh, those were the days! . . . OK . . . Yep . . . No problem, see what you can do . . . We appreciate it, sir, and who knows, perhaps we can strap those boots on for old times' sake one day? . . . Bye now, bye!'

Gaga turned to Ace with a grin.

'You'll never guess who I just got off the phone to! Mr Dean Fitzpatrick, the head of the gas network AND ex-All-Ireland football star! Would you believe I used to play for them too, once upon a time?'

Gaga chuckled to himself, and Ace could see him growing misty-eyed as he got lost in his memories.

'Er, Gaga?' Ace said, trying to bring him back to the present.

'Hmmm . . . ? Ah yes,' Gaga said, shaking the thoughts away and turning his full attention to his grandson. 'Well, he did say he's got hundreds of applications to get through, BUT, given the urgency, he's going to dig ours out on Monday and rush it through, so we can get all our fencing bought today!'

'YESSSSSS!' shouted Ace.

Just then, the doorbell rang. Ace ran to open it. It was Bear, as promised, at 9 o'clock on the dot. She was dressed in short navy dungarees over a lime-green T-shirt and her hair was separated into two tightly curled buns on top of her head.

'I'm channelling my inner Pickle and Pie today,' she said, as if she could read Ace's mind.

She paused briefly to kick off her battered old wellies before charging into the kitchen. Ace turned to follow her as Gigi called out, 'Breakfast is ready!' and within seconds the kitchen was filled with the sounds of them all loading food on to their plates. Both Ace and Bear opted for a bit of everything and washed it all down with Gigi's freshly squeezed apple juice. All that could be heard for several minutes was the clatter of plates and happy *mmm*'s and *ahh*'s as they munched their way through the delicious food. Even Gaga was quiet for once.

Once they'd finished, Ace felt energized and ready for the day.

'Right, no more sitting around,' he said, and everyone at the table sat up straighter at the sound of Ace's commanding voice. 'Let's head into town and get everything we need for the chicken coop. That's today's priority.'

They filed out of the house, down the steps and round the corner to the cherry-red motorcycles, where there was a surprise waiting for Bear. Gaga reached into one of the sidecars and picked up a brand-new helmet with a picture of a bear on the front, which he handed to her.

'Call it a little thank-you present for looking after Ace since we moved here,' said Gaga.

'Oh wow! My very own helmet! I love it – thank you!' Bear replied.

'All right, all right, enough mushy stuff from you two,' Ace said. 'Let's roll!'

Bear rode with Gigi, and Ace rode with Gaga. First stop: Baverstock Country Supplies.

★

They only needed a few bits and pieces
for the chickens at the store, but Ace had
an ulterior motive for going there first.
Ever since he'd worked out the magic of
the wellies, he'd wanted to get a pair for
Bear and some for Gaga and Gigi too.
Ace wanted to share this experience with

the rest of the Farm Squad. It would also make the farm work they needed to do over the next few weeks much quicker and easier if they could all communicate directly with the animals.

But, as he approached the shelf of wellies, his heart sank. Standing next to the rack were Isabel and Oscar, and Isabel was holding the last pair of yellow wellies! Ace was not in the mood for this encounter, but he really, really wanted those wellies, so he steeled himself and walked over. Before he could speak, Isabel turned round and spotted him.

'Oh! Ace, fancy seeing *you* here!' she sneered. 'Where's your protector – the big scary Bear?'

Ace knew Isabel well enough by now not to react. He frowned and looked at her. She was still deciding between the yellow wellies and a red pair with a black tiger-stripe pattern on. Ace knew he had to choose his next words carefully if he had any hope of walking away with the wellies he wanted.

'What's the matter, huh? Cat got your tongue?' Isabel said with a snigger.

Luckily Ace had an idea.

'I just wanted to get some more wellies. I've already got a pair of the yellow ones though, so you take those ones if you want them.'

Isabel looked Ace up and down. 'Ugh, I can't possibly consider these wellies when *he* already has them. What was I thinking?'

With a look of disgust, Isabel dropped the wellies on the floor, much to Ace's great relief.

As Isabel and Oscar walked away laughing, Bear whizzed round the corner with a flatbed trolley.

'What's wrong?' she said, as she clocked Ace's face.

He nodded in Oscar and Isabel's direction.

Instantly Bear went into protective mode, and she stared daggers at Oscar and Isabel's retreating backs. 'What did they say?' Then she called after them, 'Come back here and say it to my face!' She turned back to Ace, muttering, 'I'll show them.'

Ace looked at Bear, who had her hands on her hips and a furious expression on her face, and burst out laughing.

'Never mind them,' he said, putting the discarded yellow wellies on to the trolley. 'We've got more important things to think about right now.'

Bear didn't look convinced, but Ace's calm tone reassured her and they sped over to Gaga and Gigi at the checkout, where Gigi had a trolley-load of hay, straw and tools, along with the netting and hooks for the chicken coop. Ace ran ahead of Gaga and Bear to give Gigi the wellies.

'They're for Bear,' Ace whispered, and Gigi winked at him as she tucked them between a bale of hay and a strimmer.

With everything they needed to start work, Gaga finished loading up the motorbikes, which now looked like two cherry trees overladen with fruit.

'Right!' he said. 'Let's get lunch and then back to the farm!'

20

Ace, Bear and Gigi stepped back to survey the new chicken coop. It looked incredible. Gigi had put nameplates on individual laying pods for each chicken, as well as a perch for bedtime roosting. The roof was fully waterproofed and retractable, making egg collection much, much easier. The best part of the Strut Suite was the mini courtyard within the main building of the coop, where the chickens could have food and drink and hang out when the weather was cold or wet, if they didn't

want to be 'cooped' up all day. The Strut
Suite was also fully soundproofed, so
Charlie could crow inside it to his heart's
content all morning without ruining their
weekend lie-ins.

They were almost ready to present
it to Floss, Pixie and Agatha when Ace
remembered Bear's gift! He ran to the bike
and picked up the bag the wellies were
packed in.

With a beaming smile, Ace presented
the bag to Bear, and her face lit up like
a Christmas tree when she opened it and
saw the shiny yellow wellies inside.

'Ace! I **LOVE** them!' she squealed with
delight, hugging him so tightly round his
neck he almost collapsed!

Once Ace had steadied his legs, he smiled at Bear's reaction. 'You're a lot bossier than Kevin but, as best friends go, you're still pretty great. Try them on!' said Ace, hopeful that the wellies would work in the same way for Bear.

Sure enough, Bear's eyes widened with surprise as soon as her feet were in the wellies.

'It's all tingly! Is that the magic?!' she asked Ace, her eyes wide in wonder.

'Yep!' he said, nodding enthusiastically. 'Don't worry,' he added with a smile. 'You'll get used to it. Come on – let's show this to the chickens! *Charlie, Agatha, Pixie, Floss!*' he hollered. 'Come and see your new home!'

As expected, Charlie ran over straight away.

'Hey, Ace! Oooh, this is exciting,' the cockerel said.

Ace immediately shot a look over to Bear. *Had it worked?*

The astonishment on her face told him all he needed to know, as she finally got to hear Charlie's 'real' voice.

'Pretty cool, right?' he said, grinning.

Pretty cool indeed. For the second time in her life, Bear was speechless! Ace wished he had a camera to take a photo of her.

Gigi, on the other hand, was too busy ushering the chickens into the coop to notice Bear's stunned silence.

'There you go, girls,' she said, and a chorus of clucking came from the coop as the chickens filed in and began exploring the new space. 'I think they like it,' she added, as she gave an excited nod to Gaga who had been to get a toolbox from the shed.

Unbeknown to Gigi, this couldn't have been further from the truth ... Ace and Bear could hear exactly what the chickens were saying – and what they were hearing were a lot of complaints.

'Everything's changed,' said Floss in a panicked voice as she looked around the new coop.

'It's all different,' said Agatha in a disapproving tone.

Bear, who had recovered from the initial shock of hearing the animals talk, decided it was time for her first real conversation with an animal.

'I know it might take a little getting used to, girls,' she said, 'but why don't you try it out and then tell us what improvements are needed?'

'Exactly,' added Ace. 'Like I said before, this is your home as much as ours, so we want it to be just right for you.'

The chickens didn't reply, but they did begin walking about the coop, exploring every bit of the space and all the new inventions that Gigi had added.

Eventually Agatha stepped forward with her head held high.

In an imperious voice, she said, 'We will give you our feedback in the morning.'

Then she turned on her heel, if chickens can be said to have heels, and waddled away with as much dignity as she could muster.

Ace looked at Bear. 'I think that's probably as much as we'll get from them today. Let's call it a night.'

Bear waved goodbye to Ace and promised to be back bright and early the next day.

★

When Gigi tucked Ace into bed that night, gently kissing his forehead, she said, 'We make quite the team, don't we?'

Ace smiled. 'We've always been the best

team, Gigi – we're just getting bigger and better!'

As Ace drifted off to sleep, he dreamed of chickens strutting down a catwalk at a fashion show in some of Gaga's loudest shirts.

21

'**Ahhhh!**' Ace screamed early the next morning as he shot out of bed.

He'd woken up to the sight of two big eyes staring down at him, with a nose practically touching his. When he'd rubbed the sleep out of his eyes, he realized it was just Bear, who was standing over him with her hands on her hips as usual and her shiny yellow wellies on her feet.

She didn't acknowledge his outburst and simply said, 'Gaga and Gigi are already outside working, so you'd better get a move on, slowcoach,' before turning and walking out of the room.

Ace got ready as quickly as he could and flew downstairs. He grabbed a couple of pieces of bread, toasted them, slathered on some butter and honey, then raced out of the back door to the farmyard.

All systems were go. Gigi was in the workshop, drilling loudly, and Gaga had his radio on full volume as he cleared out the stables, the two sounds blending together in the early-morning breeze. In the background, Sybil, Ginger, Bruiser, the piglets, Pickle and Pie were all bouncing around to the music. Even Bumble gave the occasional bum wiggle, although his face remained as grumpy as ever.

Ace took it all in. He couldn't believe only a couple of weeks ago he had never met any of these animals. He didn't know what he would do without them now.

Bear was busying herself with feeding the animals, humming along to the music.

First on Ace's list for the day was to find out what the chickens had made of their night in the new coop.

'*Agatha, Pixie, Floss!*' he called, as he made his way into the pen, and he was surprised when they didn't come running out immediately.

Then he remembered one of Gigi's Strut-Suite inventions and pressed the button on the coop to retract the roof. In just under ten seconds, Ace could see right inside, and the three hens were bickering as usual! Ace coughed to alert the hens to his presence, but they ignored him and carried on arguing. Ace tried again.

'Good morning, ladies!' he said in a cheery voice.

All at once, the three hens flew at Ace in a rage.

'*Good morning?* It is not a good morning, young man,' said the hens.

'OK,' replied Ace. '*One* of you, please, tell me what's wrong.'

Pixie and Floss looked at Agatha.

'You tell 'im,' they both said in unison.

Agatha ruffled her feathers. 'This hut is, in fact, quite possibly the *worst* home we've ever had.'

Ace was disappointed, but he tried to remember that they weren't going to get everything right first time.

'We lay the best eggs in this whole district. But we can't do *that* if it's too hot or too cold. The insulation in this coop roasts us at night and freezes us during the day, so we can't lay any eggs at all ... Wait! Where are you going? How RUDE!'

The chickens continued to strut around the coop, clucking on and on about being shown more respect, until Ace reappeared ten minutes later with Gigi in tow.

'So you think there's a problem with the

temperature then, Ace?' said Gigi, looking at the chickens who had suddenly gone quiet and were peering up at them both expectantly.

'Yes, I'm sure of it,' said Ace.

Gigi didn't seem totally convinced, but she went into the pen and headed for the coop. Gigi examined the coop for several minutes, occasionally scribbling on a notepad she kept in her pocket for any brilliant new ideas. After a while, she walked back over to the gate of the pen, where Ace and an unusually quiet row of chickens were waiting patiently.

'What I can do,' continued Gigi, 'is add in a temperature regulator and some heaters. When the temperature goes below a certain level, the heaters will turn on. If it gets too hot, the roof will open up to let the heat escape and close back again when the optimum temperature has been reached. How does that sound?'

'Perfect,' said Ace, looking down at the chickens and grinning as they began clucking again.

Ace was about to follow Gigi and head back to the farmyard when he saw something out of the corner of his eye. There was a screech and a shriek and what looked like a rolling mass of black, white and brown fur, just along the fence round the pasture.

'Phantom . . . ?' Ace said to himself.

Ace's voice startled Phantom, who was

chasing a brown field mouse around the farm, and this distraction led to the cat crashing into one of the fence posts. The little brown mouse ran off squeaking, 'Yippeeee! I'm free!'

Phantom sat up, looking dazed.

Ace took this rare moment of Phantom being still to have a proper conversation with him.

'Phantom, you're a hard cat to track down. If I didn't know better, I'd say you were avoiding us,' said Ace.

Phantom started licking his paw, slowly regaining his composure.

'Well, Phantom by name, Phantom by nature,' he purred. He tried to get up to make yet another getaway, but

he couldn't walk. 'Yeeeeeoooooow!' he moaned as he tried to take a step. 'Look — I've gone and hurt my paw. It will take a while for this to heal and now I've lost my lunch too.'

Ace felt bad. 'Oh, I'm so sorry, Phantom. I didn't mean to make you crash into the fence.' Thinking on his feet, Ace made a suggestion. 'I know! Why don't you come and live in

the house with us? We can make you a
cat flap, so you can come and go as you
please, and we can feed you every day.'

Ace was sure Gaga and Gigi wouldn't
mind, but it seemed that Phantom did.
'Absolutely NOT,' he replied.
'I never live with humans! No, no, no.'

But Ace wouldn't back down until
Phantom had agreed to at least give it
a try.

'Fine,' said Phantom grumpily. 'I'll give
it a go, but absolutely no cat biscuits! I'll
leave immediately.'

Ace smiled broadly. 'No cat biscuits.
Got it.'

Phantom stopped licking his paw and
gave a slight nod of his head. 'Now, if

you'll excuse me, I've got a mouse to catch and, with this paw, it already has a head start.'

And this time, slightly slower than a flash, Phantom disappeared.

22

'Gigi?' Ace said loudly, as he opened the
door to the workshop. 'It's getting late –
I think we're going to call it a night.'

Ace stepped into the workshop with
Bear following closely behind.

'What happened here?' she said. 'It looks
like a tornado's hit this place.'

It was true – the workshop was a
gigantic mess, with boxes piled high
and tools scattered all over the floor.
The sound of clanking and grinding
and crunching was still coming from the

back of the workshop, and they were just starting to wonder where Gigi was hiding when she appeared between two teetering piles of boxes, clasping a blowtorch and wearing a welding mask. Ace was used to seeing Gigi kitted out like this, but it proved to be a bit of a shock for Bear.

'**Gahhhhhhh** – Ace!' Bear cried. 'Run! It's a monster!'

Bear courageously threw herself in front of Ace, but soon stopped when she heard Ace roaring with laughter.

She turned round, looking incredulous. 'What can you possibly be finding funny right now?'

'I think it might be you, dear,' said Gigi, as she stepped over what appeared to be

a large vacuum cleaner with a jetpack attached and lifted her mask up. 'Come on – I'll show you two what I've been working on.'

Bear was still in shock and Ace was barely able to stop laughing at Bear's panicked face and her shrill cry of 'Run!' Nevertheless, they followed Gigi deeper into the workshop, which had completely changed since they first arrived.

Gigi wrapped an arm round each of their shoulders and explained her day's work to them.

'So, today has been very productive. I've managed to remodel all the hand-held machinery so that they can be used to trim hedges, plant trees, cut grass and keep the whole farm as litter-free as possible. Ace, push that button.'

Ace walked over to a contraption that had a mechanical arm. He pushed the button as instructed and immediately the arm began moving around, snapping open and shut as if searching for something.

'Do you know what it is?' said Gigi, registering Ace's surprise. 'It's an automatic litter picker! It collects rubbish and stores it in that bag underneath it. When it's full, you can empty it, so the job is ten times easier!'

Bear and Ace beamed at Gigi's enthusiasm.

Next, she walked them over to the far wall of the workshop where there was a desk pushed up against the wall, beneath the window. On the desk were two sets of plans: one labelled 'WIND TURBINE', the other, 'BIOMASS BOILER'.

'The solar panels will be going up this coming week, as well as the wind turbine and this . . .' continued Gigi, gesturing to the beginnings of the boiler beside the desk.

The legs of the boiler were in place, as was the cylindrical shape of half its body. The other half was still in bits on the floor.

Both Ace and Bear took a look inside the complete half. It seemed to be filled with motors and pieces of metal.

'Don't worry – it's not finished, but these three pieces of equipment will make this farm fully sustainable, with all its

energy generated internally. We should be
able to produce enough power between
them to run the farm and the farmhouse.'

Ace looked inside the boiler once again.
'When this is all done, it's going to be
SO epic!'

Gigi smiled. 'Yes, it will,' she replied. 'But
that's enough show and tell for today –

you two need an early night before school tomorrow and it's already getting late. It's going to be a busy two weeks. Bear, grab your bits and I'll drop you home.'

Bear said her goodbyes to Gaga and then to Ace.

'See you in the morning,' she called to him, climbing into the sidecar of Gigi's bike, 'and don't be late!'

Ace grinned. He was never late. Well, almost never.

23

Gigi should have said it'd be a SUPER-BUSY two weeks because that's exactly what it was. She spent most of her time in the workshop, building and testing and running all the machines she'd created. The solar panels were all up and the wind turbine had been put in place. Gigi had also made a start on fixing the greenhouse and had nearly completed the weathervane that would help the whole community. She'd also batch cooked all their meals so that they could spend more time on the farm.

Meanwhile, Gaga had been busy preparing the newly refurbished stables and putting the fence up. Thankfully, he had the help of Gigi's mechanical post driver, so he got both jobs done right on time.

Ace and Bear couldn't spend all week at the farm, of course – they had to go to school – but they used all their break times and lunchtimes to brainstorm new ideas or improvements. Things were really starting to come together for the Farm Squad, but they knew there was still one man very determined to stop them.

★

Councillor Crabbington was busy doing what he did best – plotting and scheming. He'd made two secret trips to First Fruits Farm over the course of about two weeks and was enraged to see how well everything was coming together.

On Tuesday lunchtime, he sneaked through the side gate and into the yard.

So much had been done since his first visit and the family were making much better headway than he ever thought possible. To say he was unhappy about it would have been an understatement.

24

There were now seven days to go before the inspection.

★

On Day One, Gigi and Bear put the pieces together for the weathervane. It was such hard work that Gigi fell asleep lying on top of a trestle table, wearing a full-face mask and using a toolbox for a pillow and a crinkled metal sheet as a cover!

Gaga got all the planning permission for Ginger's outside space approved and set to work building what the piglets described as their very own piggy playground!

★

On Day Two, Gaga finished his work on the fence and in the stables – he'd even made special extra-large cushions for the animals to rest on, specially stuffed with thistledown. However, there were *a few* technical hitches, like Gaga putting a foot in Bumble's water bucket and tripping over the broom he'd been using to sweep up the mess, ending up with more hay on his clothes than anywhere else in the stables. Ace roared with laughter when he saw Gaga after school and told him to head back up to the house for a much-needed bath.

★

On Day Three, Gigi made delicious porridge for breakfast, with honey and blueberries and bananas. It was all the fuel she, Bear and Ace needed to program the weathervane, clean out the animals' pens and continue fixing the greenhouse. (Luckily for Bear and Ace, school was closed for a teacher-training day.) After a lunch of chicken salad sandwiches, the weathervane was linked up to the power supply on the farm.

★

On Day Four, Gaga helped Gigi by running around and setting up her new

machines. He checked to make sure the
wind turbine and the biomass boiler were
both working. Gigi then linked them to
the weathervane, which meant that the
house and the farm were now fully using
renewable energy! It was a huge box
ticked and they had no doubt it would go
down well at the inspection.

On Day Five, the greenhouse was finally complete. It had brand-new solar panels on its roof, which created extra energy that they could store for the winter months or for when they knew it might be colder than usual. Phantom, whose paw was still healing, was furious to find that Gigi had installed a bird flap so that only animals smaller than a cat could get through it.

'Stopping me from eating my lunch, as always,' Phantom muttered as he slunk away crossly.

★

On Day Six, Gaga and Ace began their morning very early by feeding all the animals before school. Gigi spent the day finishing her work on the tractor, giving it two brand-new shiny wheels. Gaga went to the shops to get spare batteries for the walkie-talkies. Then after school, everybody, including the animals, gathered together for the official unveiling of the refurbished farm! Gigi said they could celebrate by having one of her signature barbecues.

As a tired Ace headed to bed that night, he could hear whizzes, chops and swishes coming from Gaga's bedroom.

The second Ace's door had closed, Gaga emerged from his own room, looking very pleased with himself. His secret project was complete.

25

What had Gaga been up to, you ask? Well, as you know, Gaga considered himself to be a bit of a fashion icon and he had been busy sewing outfits for all the Farm Squad to wear.

'If we're a team, we need to look like one,' he said to himself as he bent over the sewing machine, his mouth full of pins.

As Ace slept deeply, Gaga crept into his room to leave his creations as a surprise for him when he woke up.

While you might have expected that Gaga was sewing for himself, Gigi, Bear and Ace, he was in fact creating something special for every Farm Squad member. Something that they could all wear on inspection day.

Gaga smiled to himself as he silently

laid a pile of neatly labelled boxes at the foot of Ace's bed, immensely pleased with his handiwork.

★

The following morning, Ace rolled out of bed and nearly fell *into* the door as he tripped over one of the little boxes that had been left in his bedroom.

Curious, he picked up the one by his foot. On it was a label that said 'Doug' – the most nervous of Ginger and Bruiser's piglets. Ace smiled as he remembered his first encounter with Doug and how he'd pooed all over his welly.

Ace's expression changed from fondness to astonishment as he opened the box and discovered Gaga's creation. It was one of the most beautiful things he had ever seen – a short, stubby little snout sock, the perfect size for Doug. It had been beautifully woven and sewn in green silk that had a purple sheen in the right light. On the front of it, there were four tiny, almost invisible, holes for breathing, and smack bang in the middle, embroidered in gold, was the image of a lightning bolt.

★

In their pen, the piglets could not contain their excitement at Gaga's gift. They all chorused at the same time:

'Wowowowowowow!'

'Can you believe we got our very own presents?'

'They're all so similar but different at the same time!'

'Now you can tell us all apart!'

'Oh, Ace,' Ginger remarked. 'Gaga's made my life SO much easier! I'll actually be able to find the right piglet for the mischief that's caused – what a relief.'

Ginger, Bruiser, Sybil and Bumble were a little more hesitant to try out the outfits Gaga had made for them.

'Give them a try! Gaga is one of the most stylish people in the world – or at least that I've ever met. If he designed it for you, it's because he knows it's going to look amazing! I think you might be surprised.'

And surprised they were. Gaga had made Bumble a beautiful cloak. It had a similar purple sheen to the piglets' snout socks, but the blanket itself was more of a deep orange colour. Bumble looked more like a majestic horse than a donkey, fit to be ridden by a knight in a fairy tale.

'Does my bum look big in this?' he asked anxiously.

'You can't even see your bum,' chuckled Pickle.

Ace couldn't help but laugh along with the goats, who both thought their outfits were fabulous! Gaga had made the two of them yellow caps that fitted snugly over their heads, with holes for their horns. Once Ace had fastened them on to their heads, the goats celebrated in the only way they knew how.

'HEAD-BUTT FI-I-I-IIGHT,'

they both bleated, before proceeding to crash into each other's heads.

Gaga had also made wing gloves for Agatha, Pixie and Floss, which were fastened with a button that went under their breasts. The wing gloves matched and blended in with their feather colours perfectly. Charlie had his own electric-blue snood, which fitted snugly round his neck feathers. Sybil had an exquisite tail sash made of white fabric, which looked like one of those funny ties you might see around the curtains of a posh hotel. When she flicked her tail, it spread out beautifully like the dress of a flamenco dancer.

Phantom hadn't been left out either. He had a pair of white booties with 'FS', for 'Farm Squad', emblazoned on each paw.

'Master Ace, these outfits are fantastic.

I'm rather impressed,' Phantom said.

'You all look unreal! I'll make sure I pass that on to Gaga, Phantom, but, before you get too comfortable in them, I have to take them back up to the farmhouse so they stay clean and safe.'

As one, the animals groaned in disappointment, but they allowed Ace to disrobe them.

On his way back to the house for breakfast, Ace couldn't help but smile. Within just a few weeks, he'd not only become friends with all these animals but he, Gigi, Gaga and Bear had completely transformed the once run-down farm. He couldn't believe they'd actually done it!

26

There was only one day to go until the inspection, and Henry Crabbington knew he had to do something, and soon, or there was no chance he would get his hands on First Fruits Farm. After pacing his office for several hours, he sat in his chair, thinking exceptionally crafty thoughts until he came up with an exceptionally crafty plan.

'Aha,' he said to himself. 'That is most certainly the most exceptionally crafty plan I have ever come up with!'

Councillor Crabbington waited until it was dark and the wind was blowing in the correct direction before he made his move. You see, he knew that if he approached the farm from the right direction – into the wind – his horrendous stench would waft *away* from the animals, meaning they would most likely stay asleep.

He parked his car in a country lane, out of sight of any late-night traffic. Then he tiptoed ever so sneakily up to the side gate to the farm, before licking his thick index finger and holding it up in the air above his head. A devious smile flashed across his face as he lifted the gate's latch; he had timed his little visit to perfection.

As he tiptoed his way towards the

animals, Councillor Crabbington couldn't believe his luck when he spied an axe by a pile of wood.

He stumbled across the chicken coop first. It took him a while to find what he was looking for, but eventually he spotted the cable that powered the Strut Suite. With a cruel smile and a swift downward swing, the councillor severed the power supply to the chicken coop in an instant.

Job done, he dropped the axe and tiptoed across the yard.

His next stop was the stables where Pickle, Pie, Bumble and Sybil were all snoring noisily. Bumble was moving around in his sleep as he always did. If you've ever seen a cow sleep, you'll know just how loud they can snore and that goats can sleep through pretty much anything.

Councillor Crabbington silently lifted up his walking stick and pulled the eagle's head off the top, revealing a set of utility tools, similar to a Swiss army knife. His kit included a mini saw, a pair of scissors, a miniature magnifying glass, a pair of tweezers, a screwdriver and a torch.

Using the scissors under the eagle's head, he sliced into Gaga's newly sewn cushions. Thanks to Sybil's delightful snoring, none of the animals were any the wiser, and the councillor let out a small chuckle to himself, as Bumble unknowingly thrashed about, causing thistledown to silently puff out of his cushions and all over the stable.

Councillor Crabbington was so pleased with himself that he could have leaped for joy, but instead he stopped dead in his tracks as he came out of the main stable doors and stood face-to-face with Gigi's incredibly impressive weathervane. He really had no idea what it was or what he should do to it, so his scheming mind recalled his grandfather's infamous saying: 'If in doubt, give it some clout.'

Councillor Crabbington returned the eagle's head to its rightful place on top of his wooden walking stick and proceeded to hit the weathervane in the hope that it would break. On his seventh strike, the weathervane began to let out

302

sparks of electricity. Relieved, Councillor Crabbington decided that he'd done more than enough damage to ensure the inspection would fail in less than twelve hours' time.

He turned to leave the farm, still taking care to be as silent as possible. As he made his way back to the lane where he had parked his car, he caught a glint of the huge greenhouse as it shone in the moonlight. Opposite the greenhouse, on the other side of the farmyard, was the Gigi-adapted green-and-yellow tractor. A sly smile crossed Henry Crabbington's lips as he approached it.

Up in the tractor's cabin, the councillor stared at the buttons, dials and levers in front of him. Finding the right one, he set pandemonium in motion with the touch of a finger. The big black wheels of the tractor began to move, then roll! Destination: the **greenhouse!**

Councillor Crabbington had left the door to the tractor's cabin wide open, so, as it hurtled towards the greenhouse, the tractor's cabin door sent bins of feed flying all over the farmyard. There was nothing to be done as the tractor punched a tractor-sized hole through the greenhouse and came to rest by the compost bin on the other side with a thud and a crash.

As if in slow motion, every pane of glass in the building shattered simultaneously and the birds that had been sleeping in its rafters flew off in sleepy confusion towards the nearest tree branch they could find.

Councillor Crabbington let out a giggle of glee as he watched the final twist in his plan reach its completion.

The farm was a total and utter mess, yet miraculously everybody in the farmhouse was still fast asleep.

27

Ace woke with a start. It was early. Very, very early. So early, in fact, that Charlie the cockerel had yet to begin his 'cock-a-doodle-doo'ing for the day. Ace rubbed his eyes and instantly felt a sense of unease come over him.

Something didn't feel right. Have you ever been so nervous that you've felt a lump in your throat? Or so anxious that you started to shake? Well, Ace, who had now become rather in tune with his new friends the farm animals, was feeling both those things at exactly the same time. He looked at his clock: 5.29 a.m. And then the wake-up call from Charlie confirmed every one of his fears.

'Cock-a-doodle-d–
CAAAAAAAAAAARK!!!' came the outrageous noise, louder than he'd ever heard it before.

★

Charlie had attempted his first call of the day while he was still half asleep. As he opened his eyes and focused on his surroundings, he quite literally could not believe what he saw. There was mess **EVERYWHERE**.

The tractor was no longer in its usual spot. The greenhouse, which he was always trying to sneak into when he went grazing, was merely a shell of steel and timber. All over the ground of the farmyard lay a sea of spilled feed, and something that looked like fluffy snow was billowing out of the stable doors.

Charlie was deeply disturbed,

especially because he realized that he didn't have the beaks of Agatha, Pixie and Floss pecking him in the side of the head, which was routine for this time of the morning. There was only one thing for it: sound the alarm!

And so Charlie proceeded to **'cock-a-doodle-doo'** until he was nearly blue in the face.

★

Ace had thrown his clothes on and raced down the stairs. He would have already been out of the door had he not spotted a folded note addressed to him on the kitchen table. He was too impatient to stop and read it though.

He stuffed it straight into his pocket but,

as he did so, he noticed that it had sat on top of a shiny white gift box. Inside was the most beautiful multicoloured gilet in bright green and red and white and royal blue, hand-sewn by Gaga. An exquisite crest had been embroidered on the collar in a fine gold thread. Beneath the gilet, Gaga had adapted the outfits for the animals: they all sported a similar crest to Ace's.

However, Ace was in too much of a hurry to examine the crest and the updated outfits. He slipped on the gilet and, in spite of his haste, he felt his chest swell a little with joy. It fitted him perfectly.

Ace picked up the animals' outfits and tucked them under his arm. He wished he'd been able to run upstairs and give both his grandparents a big hug and a thank-you kiss, but there was no time for that now.

On went his wellies, and that now-familiar tingle made him feel extraordinary once again. Little did he

know that he'd need to be extraordinary if
he was going to succeed today.

Ace raced down the path towards the
farmyard but stopped short as soon as he
saw what had happened. It was complete
chaos. The farm was a mess; all the
animals had escaped their pens and were
now wandering around the yard, talking
at the tops of their voices. He laid the
animals' outfits on the stone pillar of the
farm gate before rushing through to find
Ginger, usually the most level-headed of
all the animals, venting her disgust at a
hundred miles per hour.

'It's a disgrace! The greenhouse is
ruined! How **DARE** they! They ought
to be ashamed of themselves. Just you

wait until our Ace hears of this – he'll be outraged and . . . Dako– . . . I mean Dexter and Duke! Come back here **AT ONCE!** This is no time for you to be running off and for goodness' sake, Di– . . . I mean Daisy! Please stay away from that thing . . .'

The 'thing' Ginger had been referring to was all that was left of the humungous weathervane. It was still spitting out sparks of electricity and did not look safe at all. Phantom had not long returned from his overnight hunt and was moaning about the glass all over the ground surrounding the greenhouse.

'What a catastrophe. Think of what could happen to my dear paws!' he said, as he tiptoed round the sea of broken glass. 'And those poor birds.'

Sybil, Bumble and the goats were arguing among themselves, trying to determine, unsuccessfully, whose fault it was that all the lovely cushions had been slashed and ruined.

Ace threw his head back and let out a roaring: **'QUIIIIEEEEEEEEEET!** Please! Everybody!'

A deathly silence descended upon the farm. The only noise that could be heard was the *buzz, buzzzzz* of the broken weathervane. The time on Ace's watch was now 5.53 a.m. and in seven minutes' time they'd have four hours to get ready for the inspection.

28

Ace was on the brink of tears because he knew that the situation he faced – that they *all* faced – was virtually hopeless. He couldn't shake the feeling that their hard work had gone to waste. In frustration and anger, he stuffed his hands into his pockets and that's when he felt it – the note from the kitchen table. He read it silently, the beady eyes of every single animal firmly fixed on him, waiting for his next instruction.

To our darling grandson,

You are fantastic. You know we had our concerns about taking on the farm. It was such a big change for us, and we didn't know if we would enjoy life out in the country. But look how far we have come. Thank you for being great, and for working so hard and inspiring us oldies to always have fun! It has not been the easiest of transitions, but we are so proud of everything you have achieved. Here is a little token of our appreciation to help you ace the inspection today.

Love Gigi and Gaga

PS Try the outfits out on the animals again – we've made a few little adjustments!

Ace smiled and rolled his eyes at the terrible pun on his name, but it was just the boost of motivation he needed. This called for the best speech of his life.

Ace stood up tall and addressed the animals.

'Now listen up, Farm Squad! We've spent every day together over the last three and a bit weeks working to create a brilliant farm! This mess is a setback, but if we all help out and pull together we can get this place tidied up in time for the inspection. I know we can do it!'

The animals looked at one another, not quite fully convinced of Ace's words, but they'd built a very strong bond with him over the past few weeks and they all knew that they could depend on him.

Ace continued. 'So here's the deal: each of us is going to focus on what we're best at. It's way too early to wake Gaga and Gigi. If we work together, we can get this sorted.'

At 6.22 a.m., Ace handed each of them their gift from Gaga, this time without any protests, and set them to the task of tidying up the farm. His first job: turn off the electricity.

29

Charlie's snood looked rather odd on him, but it was actually a very clever gift from Gaga. It enabled Charlie to enhance his greatest skill – his voice!

Time was of the essence, so Ace gave Charlie one task and one task only: sing at the top of his voice when it was 9.45 a.m.

Charlie was so on edge he looked like a feathery version of the weathervane, strutting back and forth and nervously checking the watch that Ace had left with him, impatiently waiting for his moment to come.

Pickle and Pie never seemed to run out of energy and were both incredibly good at jumping about, so Ace hung a couple of nets in their horns and set them to work catching and collecting the thistledown, which was now widespread across the farm. They had such a blast frolicking in the fields that they didn't even realize how quickly they were working.

7.23 a.m.

Agatha, Pixie and Floss were understandably
still very flustered. However, Gaga's wing
gloves helped to keep their feathers from
looking unkempt – Gaga knew just how
particular the ladies were about their
appearance. Ace knew their best assets
were their beaks, so he asked them to peck
and pick up the food and debris in the
yard. He laid out some bags for them and
they took it in turns filling them up,
between laying and chattering.

★

7.57 a.m.

Bumble's strength was . . . his strength. He could carry pretty much anything and pull objects many times heavier than his own body weight. For that reason, Ace asked Bumble to help pull the tractor back into its original place. He assisted with moving the bags that had been filled by the chickens, until everything they could salvage on the ground had successfully been tidied away.

★

8.32 a.m.

Ginger and Bruiser were very quick on their feet. Ace asked them both to be responsible for overseeing the quality of work being carried out. Not only could they make sure their piglets were sticking to their own tasks, they could also point the other animals (and Ace) in the right direction just in case there was something they couldn't do or didn't know. Ace was determined to have the farm looking even better than it had before!

★

8.56 a.m.

Dexter, Daisy, Doug, Diana, Dakota and Duke, wearing the snout socks Gaga had made them, were close to having picked up all the shattered glass from the destroyed greenhouse. The piglets were notoriously mischievous, but Ace had made the task of collecting rubbish a fun competition: the piglet that collected the most glass

would get an
extra portion
of vegetables at
breakfast! Of course,
the socks also doubled as
nose protectors, meaning they
stayed safe while moving the glass around
and, boy, did the piglets love it!

Between them, the chickens and
Bumble, the yard was as spotless as it had
ever been in no time.

Sybil the cow had brilliant eyesight
and a long swishy tail that could do a
variety of jobs. Ace had given her the job
of tidying the inside of the barn. Thanks
to the lovely tail sash from Gaga, she was
able to use her tail to sweep every nook

and cranny, and her keen eyesight made sure that nothing was missed.

Once Pickle and Pie had collected all the stuffing that had come from the cushions, Sybil took it to Ace, who, in turn, refilled and sewed up the cushions. He'd been taught a basic running stitch by Gaga so, although the cushions didn't look quite brand new, they did feel comfortable again. Of course Sybil was more than happy to test their true level of comfort with her bottom once her tasks were complete.

★

9.45 a.m.

Phantom ran back and forth between the animals, delivering messages so that they could get the work done quicker.

They were just finishing up the final bits of their tasks when Charlie called out a deafening **'COCK-A-DOOOOOOODLE-DOOOOO!'**

★

9.49 a.m.

It was only a matter of minutes before Gigi and Gaga were out of the house and running down to the farm.

'Gaga! Gigi! I'm so glad you're finally here,' cried Ace. 'We've had a nightmare overnight!'

Ace told his grandparents about what he'd woken up to, how the farm had been ruined but how he and the Farm Squad had done everything they could to put it all back together. The two grandparents could not believe their ears. They also couldn't believe what Ace had managed to achieve while they were still asleep in the house.

'The only thing we couldn't fix was the weathervane,' Ace reported. 'The power is still off.'

Gigi frowned and dashed back to the house to get her laptop. Meanwhile, everybody, including the animals, gathered round Ace.

★

9.51 a.m.

Gigi explained that the vane had been pretty badly damaged but that, if she could reset and reprogram the system, she might be able to get it up and running for the inspection.

Gaga turned the power back on
and Gigi began tapping away on her
keyboard. It seemed like her repairs
had worked, as the vane was no longer
buzzing. She slammed down the lid of her
laptop just as Bear appeared in the yard,
bumping fists with Ace to say hello.

'Guess who I've just seen outside the
gate,' she whispered urgently to Gaga and
Gigi. 'Councillor Crabbington!'

30

Henry Crabbington tapped his walking stick on the farm gate.

'**AAAHEM**, excuse me, is Ace –'

The councillor stopped abruptly mid-sentence because he could not believe his eyes. The farm had been totally transformed since he had left last night. He stared in disbelief at Ace, Bear, Gaga and Gigi. How on earth had they done it? His already flushed face was getting redder and redder by the minute, until the inspector, who was standing beside Crabbington, looked at him in alarm.

'Councillor, are you quite well? You've gone a very strange colour. Perhaps you should go home?'

Crabbington made an effort to calm down and forced himself to smile at the inspector through gritted teeth.

'I feel . . . perfectly well, er, thank you,' he grunted.

The inspector looked unconvinced, but he turned to the Farm Squad and introduced himself.

'I am Mr Livingston Bliss. Mr Henry

Crabbington, who is also the local councillor for this area, has nominated you for inspection. He has said that this farm is, and I quote: "in exceptional disrepair and should be dealt with in accordance with section 17.8 (dd) of the Local Property Ownership Act. This act authorizes a property to be put up for sale if it does not meet the necessary criteria to remain in the possession of its owner." Who, may I ask, is the proprietor here?'

Ace stepped forward, feeling as nervous as he did the first time he'd introduced himself to Councillor Crabbington.

'I am,' he said.

Mr Bliss squinted down at Ace over the

top of his spectacles. 'Very well – please show me the farm.'

Ace swallowed nervously and directed Mr Bliss into the farmyard, gaining more and more confidence as he showed the inspector the facilities. All the animals were in their own areas, and the barn was spotless; Mr Bliss commented on how vibrant – and indeed how unusual – the cushions were and the fact that the pens were neat and tidy. Pickle and Pie were on their best behaviour, as Ace showed the inspector the energy-saving aspects of the biomass boiler inside the stables.

They continued to the field where the solar panels and wind turbine were. There, Gaga explained how much power they could generate, and Mr Bliss said he was incredibly impressed.

The piglets behaved themselves too – well, mostly, and Ginger and Bruiser took great pride in running through the woodland they now called home – complete with a wallow pit.

Ace took a peek at the inspection sheet and could only see big green ticks. He was just starting to relax – but then Mr Bliss's eyes alighted on the greenhouse.

Taking a closer look, he could see that there was no glass in the framework. He shook one of the door frames and said, 'I can see that panes of glass are missing from this structure, which could potentially be dangerous.'

Before Ace could reply, Councillor Crabbington piped up. '**EXTREMELY** dangerous if you ask me.' He said this with a smug glance towards Ace.

Mr Bliss put a big red cross on the sheet, next to the heading 'Outbuildings', and scribbled a short note in his very scribbly, very unreadable handwriting.

Gigi showed Mr Bliss the farm
machines and there wasn't a shadow
of a doubt in her mind that he would
be thoroughly blown away. And blown
away Mr Bliss most definitely was!
Never before had he seen such an array
of useful machines, making work around
the farm a doddle. More green ticks were
added to the sheet.

Mr Bliss did, however, notice quite a
few scratches and a rather large dent
in the tractor. Although the tractor had
been moved from the greenhouse by the
animals, they had not had time to ask
Gigi to fix it. In any case, mending it was
not a quick or easy task, and so they all
gulped nervously when Mr Bliss said to

Gaga, 'Please could you start the tractor for me, Mr O'Sullivan?'

Gaga walked towards the tractor, and, as he put the key into the ignition and turned it, Ace's heart sank. The tractor wouldn't start! He knew that this would be another red cross.

'Mr Bliss, as you know,' said Bear, 'Mr O'Sullivan is quite new here so he's still learning how to operate machines like the tractor. Can I show you how it works?' She smiled politely.

With a curt nod from Mr Bliss, Bear jumped up into the cabin of the tractor and rustled around. After what felt like a lifetime, suddenly the tractor roared into life! Bear leaped down from the cabin

and winked at Gaga. Mr Bliss smiled and
made no further comment as he wrote
down more notes.

'*Remind me to show you how to hot-wire
the tractor later*,' Bear whispered to Gaga.
'*It's always handy if the key doesn't work!*'

Ace was still feeling nervous. He

desperately wanted to tell Mr Bliss that there had been a series of mysterious accidents overnight, leaving the farm in a terrible mess. He wanted him to know how, in just over four hours, he and the Farm Squad had tidied everything up. Instead he struggled to put on his brave face again before walking towards the chicken coop.

Thankfully, full power had returned to the coop and the ladies were laying big, beautiful brown eggs as the inspector peered in. Charlie was finally silent and taking a nap in the Strut Suite, which the inspector had to admit was 'state of the art'. This resulted in a big green tick on the inspection sheet, as everyone walked into the middle of the yard towards the humungous weathervane.

It had stopped buzzing but was still throwing out erratic sparks of electricity. Luckily the inspector didn't feel it was necessary to investigate such a complex-looking piece of equipment and opted instead to begin his debrief of the farm. Ace, Gaga, Gigi, Bear and the animals all breathed a **huge sigh** of relief.

'Well, this farm certainly has the potential to be great,' began Mr Bliss. 'However, there are some areas of concern that I cannot ignore. The greenhouse is currently unsafe, and I will need to return to ensure that its safety has been established. Every working farm should also have safe working machinery and, as demonstrated by the fact that the tractor would not start with the turn of a key, this is also a huge concern.

'Having said that,' he continued, 'almost every other aspect of the machinery is cutting-edge, and I must commend you, Ms George, on your innovation. Similarly, I have never seen the living areas of a farm so spotlessly clean and, Mr O'Sullivan, you have added some fantastic decorative touches.'

The mood among the animals was becoming increasingly positive but, as they listened intently to the inspector, the weathervane began to shudder. And shudder. And then stop!

Mr Bliss looked up. A quizzical look crossed his face. He turned to Councillor Crabbington.

'What on earth was that?' he asked him.

Gigi took control. 'We're just putting some finishing touches to our weathervane, which will be able to give us accurate weather reports four weeks in advance to help us with all the future plans we have for the farm –'

The councillor cut Gigi off. 'It looks like a safety hazard to me – might be worth investigating, eh, Mr Bliss?'

Throughout the visit, Mr Bliss had heard these snide comments from the councillor and he'd had enough.

'Yes, thank you, Councillor. I will

344

decide what needs investigating and what does not.' Mr Bliss composed himself and continued. 'Master Ace, your animals are all impeccably behaved, and I have noted the great care you and Bear take with them, which leads me to believe that, with a little extra work, this farm will indeed be one of a kind.'

Those words were exhilarating to hear, but no one dared celebrate until they had absolute confirmation. The whole farm seemed to hold its breath. Mr Bliss ripped the top sheet of paper from his pad.

'I hereby declare that this farm has *passed* the inspection and will remain in the possession of its proprietor, Master Ace Sinclair.'

The whole farm erupted at the word 'passed'. Bumble began braying and kicking, and Sybil let out a deep, throaty 'moooo' as she voiced her congratulations. The goats did a goaty frolic to show just how happy they were for Ace, while Charlie, Agatha, Pixie and Floss hurriedly emerged from their coop to see what all the fuss was about.

Gaga picked Ace up and whirled him round in his arms.

'You did it!' cheered Gigi, punching the air.

'Yeah, Ace, we knew you could!' said the piglets in a chorus.

Everybody was so happy, but the frown on Councillor Crabbington's face only deepened. He had to admit that all the work Ace had put in was quite astonishing.

As Councillor Crabbington sloped off to his car, he muttered to himself, 'Unbelievable! How did they do it? I made it practically impossible for them to pass this inspection.'

Both Ace and Bear overheard his comment and immediately pounced on him at the same time.

'What did you just say?' they chorused.

The penny finally dropped for Ace, who knew in that instant without a

347

doubt that it must have been Crabbington who'd deliberately tried to sabotage the inspection.

'**I KNEW IT!** It was **YOU** all along! **YOU** did all that damage!' shouted Ace, filling with rage. 'Why would you even do something like that?!' he asked the councillor, crossing his arms firmly in front of him.

'I-I-I-I . . . don't have to justify or explain myself to the likes of you,' Councillor Crabbington replied defiantly.

Before they could probe him any more, Councillor Crabbington tucked his walking stick up underneath his arm, turned on his heel and marched through the farm gate.

31

Once the farm had finally shed its visitors, Ace ran to his grandparents and hugged them both as tightly as he could.

'Gaga and Gigi, thank you both so much for your belief in me and for all your help! You really are the best and you have NO idea how helpful your note was to us all tidying up this morning!'

'Ace, we are so proud of you,' said Gaga. 'You've proven just how hard-working and resilient you are, and you should be very proud of yourself too.'

Ace looked for Bear to thank her as well, but she was nowhere to be seen.

'Where on earth is Bear?' he said. 'How does she always manage to disappear at the most important moments?'

It was then that Bear walked through the side gate with a massive grin on her face. Behind her was . . .

'KEVIIIIIIIIIIIIIN!' Ace shouted in amazement. 'What are . . . ? How did you . . . ?'

He threw his arms round Bear and Kevin, his two best friends.

'Well, best friends do nice things for each other,' explained Bear, 'and I knew that you'd pass the inspection with flying colours. So I made you this,' she said, handing him a carefully drawn map of First Fruits Farm – with *all* its new additions! Bear went on, '*And*, with Gaga and Gigi's help, I organized for Kevin to come up and celebrate with us all as an extra surprise for you.'

'Thank you, thank you, thank you!' said Ace, throwing his arms round both of his best friends *again*, so tightly they almost choked.

'Yeah, she certainly doesn't take no for an answer, does she?' replied Kevin. 'But, as best friends go, she's pretty cool! Anyway, I've missed a football tournament to get here, so please let go of me and we can play a little celebratory game for old times' sake? What do you say?'

Ace laughed, released his grip on them both and ran after Kevin, who, unsurprisingly, produced a football from his backpack within seconds.

Gaga and Gigi beamed at each other.

'You know what this calls for, don't you?' said Gaga.

'A party!' replied Gigi. And, with that, she and Gaga hurried up to the house to blast some party tunes and prepare a

brunch feast of gargantuan proportions –
this time *with* eggs, fresh from the farm!

Kevin shouted up to Gigi. 'I know it's
still early, but **pleeeeeeease** can we
have some spare ribs on the menu?'

Gigi chuckled. 'I'll see what I can do –
just be up at the house in half an hour!'
she shouted.

★

After an energetic kickabout, Ace told Kevin and Bear to run ahead of him and grab some food. He had one more thank you he wanted to make and that was to the animals: his very own Farm Squad.

He gathered them all behind the stable block – even Phantom had found a beam to climb and perch on while he listened to Ace addressing the group.

'I just want to say **WELL DONE** to you all. I can't believe we managed to pull this off, but it just goes to show teamwork makes the dream work! Thank you, all!' he said, as Doug nibbled on the right toe of his yellow wellies and rubbed his snout on him.

'**Hear, hear,**' shouted Bruiser from the wallow pit. '**Three cheers for Ace!**'

And the animals all whooped and hollered and cheered for Ace.

At 11.24 a.m. that Saturday morning, Ace finished laying out treats for the animals, giving them an extra scratch or pat to show his appreciation for all their support. So much had changed since he'd received that letter from his Great-Uncle Hakim's lawyer. As he heard the animals chomping with delight and the pumping tunes coming out of Gaga's speakers, Ace Sinclair knew that he was truly home.

He'd also finally worked out what he was best at, and that was running the Farm Squad!

He wandered up the path to the house, thinking about what delicious treats Gigi had prepared for brunch. Suddenly, out of nowhere, a flash of lightning streaked through the sky. A billowing white cloud began to form around the top of the weathervane, before it spat out the tiniest of white flakes.

As the flake hit the tip of Sybil's rather large pink nose, she lifted her head and uttered, 'My, my, is it snowing?'

The weathervane shuddered and stopped, shuddered and stopped. Then it shuddered and stopped a third time. It had indeed begun to snow. Which would have been OK had it not been the middle of June.

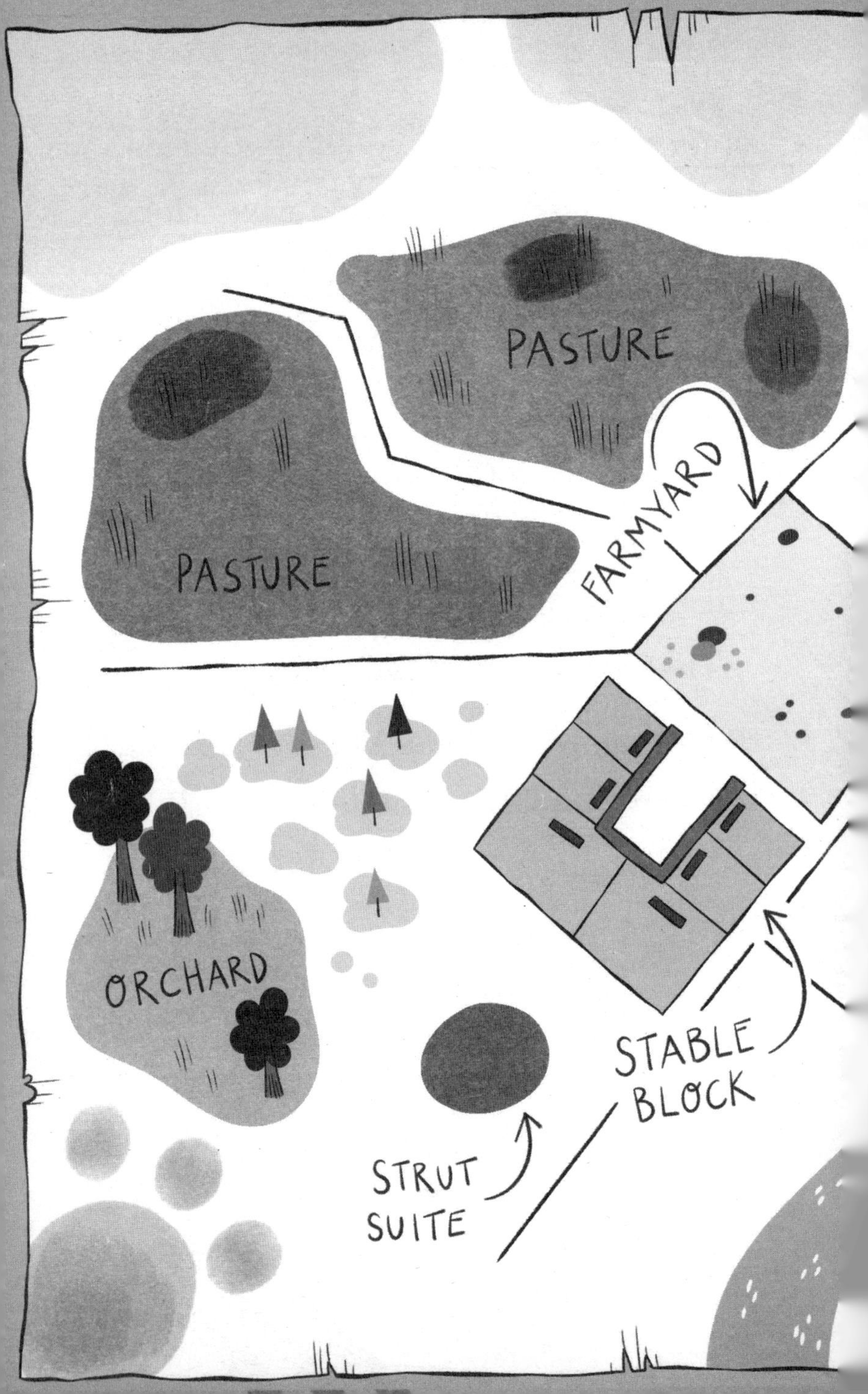
PASTURE
PASTURE
FARMYARD
ORCHARD
STABLE BLOCK
STRUT SUITE

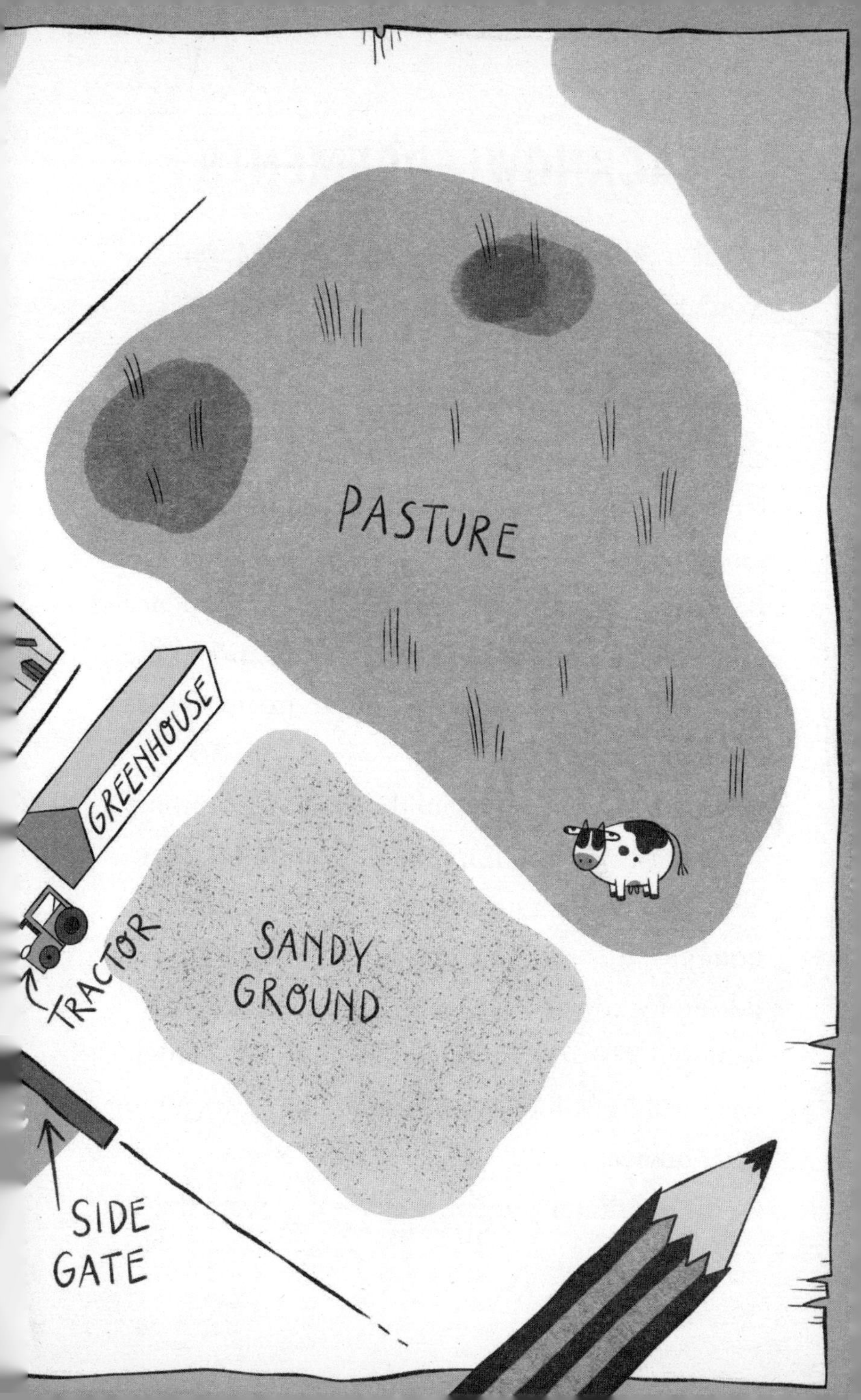
PASTURE
GREENHOUSE
SANDY GROUND
TRACTOR
SIDE GATE

ACKNOWLEDGEMENTS

What a difference eight years makes! Many won't know the challenges that faced the making of this book, and although there were plenty of trials, numerous errors and an abundance of changes, Ace and the Animal Heroes is a book series that owes much thanks and gratitude to many people.

To my wife, Chloe, I appreciate your patience while I wrote this book; thank you for giving me the time and space I needed, not to mention the drive to complete it.

I want to give a special thank-you to authors Rachel Bright and Tom and Giovanna Fletcher. You have no idea how much encouragement you gave me – to pick up my incomplete project during lockdown and keep going until it found its home. The insightful conversations we shared were truly invaluable, and I really am grateful for your advice.

To my literary agent, Steph – you were the

first agent I spoke to; for one reason or another, we weren't able to work together initially, but we got there in the end! Thanks for your time spent reading *Ace and the Animal Heroes: The Big Farm Rescue* in the early days, and for all your work partnering me with Puffin.

To my fabulous editor at Penguin, Carmen, thank you for believing in this project enough to publish it and also making it much more readable!

To Becka Moor, who's brilliantly brought all my descriptions to life through her drawings – thanks for making the Farm Squad look amazing.

To Alice, Izzy, Wendy, Lowri, Josh, Arabella, Kat, Lizz, Adam, and all the friends, relatives, agents, writers and individuals that contributed knowingly and unknowingly – there are too many of you to name, but if you've been involved with this process over the last eight years, you should fully accept my thanks! Lastly, to my uncle Hakim – I hope that wherever you are you will be proud to see this story continue your quest for adventure. Here's to the next chapter.

Look out for Ace's
next adventure!

ACE and the
ANIMAL HEROES
2

Coming spring 2024